The BIG CRYOSLEEP

an Alan Blades adventure

Nate Streeper

Listic Publishing

Santa Barbara, California, USA

ISBN-13: 978-0-578-78446-5 (Paperback)

Published by: Listic Publishing
Santa Barbara, California, USA
hello@listicpublishing.com

Cover Artwork by Dharitha "Dee" Pathirana @art_of_dee

Printed and bound in the United States of America
First Edition, 2020

Dedicated to my fellow writers.
The struggle is real.

Alan's first five rules for being a good private detective:

#1: Always trust your gut.

#2: Keep what you know to yourself.

#3: Don't trust anybody.

#4: Never leave your vibroknuckles on a gaming table.

#5: Never forget that being a private detective means you are a badass.

1

Crackdog Stand

10 p.m. found me scarfing down crackdogs at Ernie's vending cart.

I'd spent the past hour there, on the street corner, staking out a nearby apartment complex on account of a cheating wife. Only this wife's cheating was more traditional than most. Rather than hooking up with an arguably benign sexdoll, she was hooking up with a real person. Allegedly, at least. That's what I was here to discover, whether her husband was observant or paranoid.

I was getting tired of standing. And Ernie's banter notwithstanding, I was getting bored.

Listic, my fritzy Occipital Roaming Bot, floated above the entrance to the apartment complex, ready to record the comings and goings of its residents and visitors. Merely a cybernetic eyeball, she was hard to notice, as long as she remained perfectly still. And didn't zip around. Like she was doing. Right now.

"Listic!" I whispered a shout, as if such a thing was possible. I knew she could hear me, even though a human at that distance wouldn't have been able to. "Listic, stop moving!"

She stopped bouncing around and turned her glowing blue iris toward me. It dimmed in response to my scolding, the equivalent of a seven-year-old slumping her shoulders and pouting after being told to stop grabbing things in an Ultramart. She snapped back into position in a huff.

She was as bored as I was.

Ernie refilled his napkin dispenser. "I thought you was gonna get that thing fixed."

"What, my ORB? Me too. Bone was supposed to track down the Manic Virus antidote for me months ago."

Ernie dispensed with the dispenser beneath the cart's cluttered countertop. "Speakin' of things not happening... Business. As in there ain't any. You've been my only customer the past hour. I gotta pack up, Alan. Time to call it a night."

"You can't go yet, Ernie. If you leave, I'm no longer a crackdog customer. I'm just some asshole standing on the street corner. It'll blow my cover. Not to mention Rule #6."

"Rule #6?"

"For being a good private detective: When performing a stakeout, do it near a food source."

"Hey listen, you're a great guy and all Alan, but late night stakeouts? That's kinda your thing. My thing's sellin' crackdogs to the populace, and right now, there's no populace. Long as you keep feedin' me goola, I'll keep feedin' you dogs. Otherwise..."

"Okay, okay. I'll take another one."

Ernie brushed his hands together. "Comin' right up."

"With extra—"

"Extra relish. I know, I know."

A SmartCan hovered over the moment I'd finished the last bite of my previous dog. I tossed the wrapper in. Ever since being incorporated into the newly minted Victorian Cluster last year, Fillion had gotten more serious about keeping its streets clean.

The air too, for that matter—the terraformers along the dome's border had gotten major upgrades due to the reallocation of Cluster-tax, allowing all of us to breath a bit easier. Instead of needing to wear a mask the majority of the week, we now got to walk around like we were terrestrial natives. Of course, some people still wore them out of habit, but I was happy to leave mine hanging on the wall hook at home. Or in my office. I had an office, now. Anyway, I hated the damn things as much as Ruvellians hated underwear.

Not only was Fillion smelling better, it was growing. Two more environmental domes bubbled up near the downtown district, their function more suburban in nature.

Once the houses were finished, the habitrails between the domes would hum with hovercars and commuters. People were beginning to think of this planet as a desirable residence rather than merely an interstellar way station or a congregation of lowlifes.

Not that I was concerned about losing business. If there was one thing I learned as a Private Detective, or prior to this, as a GalactiCop, it was illicit doings are rarely a surface-level phenomenon.

There's always dirt beneath the concrete; the concrete merely masks it. Start digging anywhere, eventually, you'll hit the dirt.

These days? I rotated a full roster of cases. Some clients were even on a waiting list. My involvement in what became known in the newsfeeds as the Victorian Pirate Encounter made me something of a local celebrity. Turned out if you helped lock up a syndicate crime lord and a dirty politician en route to an undiscovered planet occluded by space pirates, people decided you're good at your job.

Which basically meant I was inundated with cheating spouse cases.

I was two bites into my latest gut buster when a tall brunette wearing a midnight blue evening gown and bright orange lipstick rounded the corner and walked right up to the crackdog cart. I recognized her instantly, but acted like I didn't.

"One with no relish, please."

Ernie balked. "Wait, did you say no relish?"

"I did."

"Listen, lady, I don't know if you've ever had one of these before, but the relish, it's kind of a thing around here, you know?"

"Fine. Relish, no relish, I don't care. Just give me one."

"You got it."

I looked across the street and tried to act casual, like Any Guy on a corner enjoying his food.

"You the private dic on my ass?" the brunette said without looking at me.

"Excuse me?"

"The detective. The one my husband hired to watch my every fucking move."

"I don't know what you're talking—"

"Uh huh. Listen, you're Alan Blades, okay? That famous detective guy. And I know my husband hired a detective, because the idiot was dumb enough to pay for one out of our mutual goola account. Line item said 'detective agency.' So I figure, seeing as how he hired a detective, and you're a detective, and you're standing outside the place of the guy I'm screwing, well, you're on my ass. Here, this one's on me."

She handed me the crackdog she'd ordered.

"No really, I don't need another—"

"Take it. And give my husband's money back on account of me catching you catching me. It's my goola too—I make more than that loser does, so most of the goola he's paying you is mine, and I want it back."

Listic jetted over to my shoulder. "I think she's onto us, boss."

"You think?"

"Anyway," the woman went on, forcing her newly purchased food into my free hand and thus making me look like a double-fisting contestant in a crackdog competition, "you go ahead and tell Sal. Yeah, sure, I'm cheating on him—seeing as how he won't stop flirting with my cousin, and god help me if the two of them aren't fucking every other Fillday while I'm at Toga Yoga. Like it isn't obvious. This is payback, bitch. So yeah, I suppose if you want to keep the goola he paid you, maybe you could look into my cheating skank of a cousin situation instead and insert my name on your invoice. Assuming that isn't a conflict of interest, or anything."

We stared at each other for a moment. Listic blinked.

"Well, I'm glad I stayed open for this," Ernie said.

"Yep," Listic said. "She's onto us."

My quarkphone rang. I handed the extra crackdog back to the brunette, pulled the phone out of my jacket pocket, and looked at the display. 1BX589034.

Alice.

"Well?" Orange Lipstick said.

"Hold on, I gotta take this."

I flipped open my phone. "What's up, Alice?"

The brunette folded her arms and huffed. But she didn't go anywhere.

"Oh, it's his ex-wife's sister," Ernie told the brunette. "She's in the GalactiCop Academy."

"Uh huh."

"Alan told me he promised to be there for her if she ever needed anything. She's a real go-getter, that Alice. Got this dynamite hair. Dark blue. Anyway, she'd called a half-hour ago, said she'd call back."

"Gotta say, this is too much backstory."

"Excuse me," I said, walking away from Ernie's narrative. "Alice?"

"Hey Alan." Her voice sounded metallic over the quarkphone. I was still getting used to the device—not only how it operated, but how it meant I no longer needed to align my interstellar communication with the opening and closing of the commercial subgates that orbited our planet. Quarkphones tapped into the omniquarks of the ansible network, and as such, were capable of sending and receiving calls with any other quarkphone at any time. But to be honest, as convenient as it was, part of me didn't like being available at all times. I kind of missed the days when I'd need to be home to receive calls on my subphone. I don't know, call me old fashioned.

"What's up?" I asked.

"I don't know if I can do this."

"You can do this."

"No, for real. I mean, the educational stuff, memorizing the laws and cluster codes and all that, I can handle that. After four years of college, that part's a walk in the park. By the way, what's with all those hybrid-monkey laws in Quartermast?"

"Yeah, they have a whole thing regarding hybrid-monkeys there."

"No hybrid-monkeys allowed in the streets after dusk? Hybrid-monkeys aren't allowed to eat raisins from waxed boxes less than five cubic ounces? What the hell is that about?"

"They must have had some kind of specific monkey-raisin incident."

"Monkey's aren't allowed to do shit in Quartermast."

"I know. So it sounds like you've got all the monkey ordinances memorized. What's going on, then?"

"It's the fucking exercise. I thought I was in shape, but what they're asking us to do is ridiculous. You know they have this wall? A wall, with like, tiny crevices in it."

"The Wall of Death."

"Yes, the wall of death. That one. They want us to climb over the Wall of Death. Before we run ten miles. Like, that's the warm up."

"It's good practice."

"Practice for what? For all the climbing of the walls? How often do people need to climb walls?"

"When you're a GalactiCop? You'd be surprised."

"So how many walls have you had to climb since the Academy?"

I had to stop and think about it. "No, wait. Yep. Yep, there was in fact a wall I almost needed to climb once. I was chasing a perp."

"So did you climb it?"

"No. I went around it."

"See? That's what I'm fucking talking about. All you need to do is go around it. Why would you ever climb a wall in real life?"

"I think you're missing the point. The point is to get in shape."

"Well I have discovered I am not in shape."

"Like I said, the point is to get in shape."

I noticed another guy approach the vending cart and ask Ernie a question while I paced around talking to Alice. For business being dead, the street corner was sure humming now.

The guy looked familiar. I covered the mic on my quarkphone. "Hey Listic, where do we know him from?"

She zipped over to my free ear and whispered. "Define 'know.'"

Useless.

Rather than handing over a crackdog, Ernie responded to the guy's inquiry by pointing him in my direction. When he looked straight at me, I recognized him: One of The Boneyard's bouncers. He lumbered my way.

"...Besides, don't GalactiCops end up getting fat, anyway? Like after all this bootcamp nonsense, they never make you do it again. You can sit in your patrol car and stuff yourself with gonuts. What's with that? And what's with the—"

"Hey Alice, hold on."

I lowered the quarkphone from my ear. She kept talking while the bouncer cut in. The man's voice didn't sync with his figure. More like a baby voice. "Hey Blades? Bone has a situation he's hoping you can help him with."

"What kind of situation?"

"The murdering kind."

Alice interrupted herself and shouted. "Wait, did some guy say murder? You have a murder case?"

"Who killed who?" I asked.

"One of the dolls. Went berserk, killed a John. Tore his—"

"Okay, right. So why not call the GalactiCops?"

"Oh, the place is swarming with GCs. That's the problem. Bone's freaking out."

I could let it go. Bone and I were pretty square, as far as favor trades were concerned. But that's the thing about trading so many favors with someone. Eventually, you stop doing it because you owe them. You do it because they've become your friend. "Alright, I'll check it out." I held the phone back up. "Alice, I have to go."

"Wish I had a murder case."

"Well, first you have to climb the wall."

"Whatever, Alan."

"You can do this. I'll talk to you later." I hung up. The bouncer turned and I followed him. Orange

Lipstick threw up her hands as we passed. "What, that's it? You're not taking me up on my offer? I'll throw down an extra hundred goola if you tail my husband instead of me."

"Listen, he's not fucking your cousin."

"And how would you know?"

"Because I looked into him. Before I looked into you. I looked into both of you. Your twenty-fifth's coming up, right?"

"Our twenty-fifth what?"

"Wedding anniversary."

"Sure. Next month. Like it's gonna happen, now."

"He's been meeting up with your cousin on Filldays—"

"I knew it!"

"—so she could help him with your twenty-fifth wedding anniversary. That Earth flower you like so much, the one that's so hard to grow out here..."

"Daisies?"

"Daisies. Your cousin's been growing them in that watchamacallit of hers, that... That greenhouse. It's like a terradome under the terradome. Hundreds of daisies. He drops by to tend to them every other week, wants to do his part. Tills the soil, waters them, whatever he can do. Your cousin's the botanist, but she's gotten a kick out of sharing her passion with him. Idea is to fill your bedroom with the flowers on your anniversary."

"Fuck." She took a bite of the crackdog and stared across the street. "Daisies."

"And yeah, it's true. Or half true, what you've gathered. They've gotten closer, bonded over the whole thing. But I don't think they've slept with each other.

Not yet. Only I'd be lying if I didn't admit it was possible. I believe him when he says he hasn't, but you know, he thinks you're sleeping with this other guy, which you are, and the whole thing's spun out of control..."

She swallowed, then sighed, then reluctantly nodded her head.

"Just answer this," I said. "Honestly. Do you still love him? Do you still love your husband?"

"I do." And I could tell she meant it.

"Then I'm giving you a choice."

The bouncer cleared his throat. "Hey Blades, we better get—"

"Hold on." I held my index finger up and gave him a look that let him know I didn't care how big he was, I'd do things at my own pace. He backed down, and I turned back to Orange Lipstick. "I'm giving you a choice. I go back and tell him you've been sleeping with someone else, or I go back and tell him you love him, because as far as I'm concerned, they're both true."

The SmartCan hovered over to her and she dropped the remainder of the dog in it. "Neither," she said. "I'll take it from here." She turned around and walked back in the direction she came from.

Sometimes I make my money by digging up dirt. Sometimes I make it by marriage counseling.

"Alright big guy, let's go solve a murder. Want a crackdog?" I unloaded mine into the bouncer's hand as we walked toward The Boneyard. "Later, Ernie."

"Yeah, sure. See you tomorrow, Alan." He shut off the holograph floating above his vending cart. "We'll do this again."

Listic floated over to my head. "Hey, boss?"

"Yeah?"

"It's official. You've got your mojo back."

"Thanks."

"Hey boss?"

"Yeah?"

"What do you think that lady's gonna tell her husband?"

"I guess we'll find out."

"Hey boss?"

"What."

"What do you think the crazy sex doll tore off the John?"

"I don't want to know."

The bouncer swallowed the last bite of the crackdog. "She tore off his penis."

Listic stopped asking questions after that.

2

Going AWOL

The Boneyard was only four blocks from Ernie's corner. Hovercars zipped by as we got closer to the nightlife scene, most of them yellow-checkered Youbers giving rides home to the inebriated or rides downtown to those hoping to inebriate. We approached my new office en route. I pointed it out to the bouncer.

"That's me," I said, gesturing toward the second floor of a Fillion brownstone in the business district.

"What d'ya mean?"

"That's my place. My office." I was very proud of this. Up until recently, I'd been working out of my apartment building. Or meeting clients in cafes. Or bars. Or sexdoll brothels.

The bouncer stopped and looked up. "Where?"

"Oh, for... Up there! Right there! The second floor, where the window is."

Even I had to admit, the brownstones tended to blend together. If there was one thing Fillion provided plenty of resources for, it was brick production. The early urban architects took advantage of it a little too readily, in my humble opinion. Tour guides would tell you downtown Fillion was "Metapostmodernish New England Style." But I say a brick is a brick.

"You need a sign," the bouncer said in his annoying baby voice.

"I have a sign! Look. Okay, wait. Take a few steps back." We stepped back together. "There, now look. A sign." I folded my arms. I was really excited about this sign: Alan Blades, Private Investigator. No case too big. No case too small. And there was a picture of my face.

"Huh. Nice mug. Good likeness, strong sex appeal. Square jaw, keen eyes... It's like you, but better looking."

"Thank you?"

"But still. It's flat against the wall. How's anyone supposed to see that as they walk by?"

"They can see it from here."

"Who's gonna see it from here? We had to walk over to this exact spot to see it. The edge of the sidewalk. You want people to be able to see your sign from the middle of the sidewalk. You need one of those signs that stick out. A hanging sign. Like from a pole."

I stared forlornly at my wall sign. I was getting schooled by a bouncer. And he was absolutely right. "I admit, it's harder to see when it's this dark out, but—"

"Or maybe like one of those," he said, pointing at the holographic neon sign bouncing around in midair above The Chicken Shack. "Or one of those," he said, pointing further down the street at the Chinese lightning dragon that weaved among the pedestrians before rocketing toward the entrance of The Hungry Pagoda and exploding into rainbow flames.

"I was going for something a little more understated."

"That much comes across."

A block further and we reached The Boneyard. Or at least, we reached its perimeter. It had a flat sign, by the way. Of course, it was a hard building to miss, its straight up phallic design making it impossible to overlook. Three GalactiCop hovercars were parked out front, at those odd angles that ignore actual parking spots since cops can park anywhere they fucking want. The sidewalk was packed with Boneyard evictees and looky-loos while the investigation commenced. Three cars meant six officers, two of whom remained at the building's entrance, keeping people out. Back on New Gaia, where I was a GC, we used to toss out some force barriers, maybe even shock barriers, if the crowd seemed aggressive. But out here on Fillion, the GC didn't have all the bells and whistles at their disposal.

The black unmarked homicide detective's hovercar had yet to show. This could mean one of two things. Given the killing was supposedly conducted by a sexdoll, the incident may have been called in as an accident as opposed to a murder. Either that, or it was a busy night for homicide.

"Bone said you'd know where to find him," the bouncer said. He must have been referring to the secret multisex bathroom exit in the back alley. "He said he'd be there at 10:35."

"Listic, what time is it?"

"10:33 and 48 seconds. 49 seconds. 50 seconds. 51—"

"Listic, Off." Her eye faded and she floated down to my hand. I pocketed her. "Alright, I'll swing around back. You create a diversion."

"What kind of diversion?"

"You're a doorman, right? Say you're back to finish your shift."

"What, and like try to convince the GC to walk away?"

"Yeah. That's the idea."

"But they won't. I'll get stuck there, arguing with them about it. They might even bring me in for questioning."

"That's the idea. The arguing, the questioning... That's what 'covering for me' means."

"Oh," he said. "Well when you put it that way..."

He walked into the crowd toward the entrance. As soon as the officers confronted him, I snuck around to the back.

Two entrepreneurial homeless guys, Rutger and Howard, were at their usual posts, wearing their usual tattered brown and green trenchcoats. Homeless, that is, if you discounted their dilapidated enviro-tent further down the alley, which at the moment looked even more dilapidated than usual. As far as covering for people's backdoor exits was concerned, these two back alley dwellers were masters. Any Johns sneaking out the back of The Boneyard could toss a goola chip in their beggar's bowl in exchange for a distraction. The duo would cover the escapee by blocking the alley and telling any unwanted intruders a slew of dumb knock knock jokes. Everybody wins.

"Knock knock," Rutger said as I rounded the corner. He'd taken to shaving his head, giving him the appearance of the Buddha.

"It's only me, Rutger."

"Alan!" Howard said. "Been awhile, man. Weeks." His shaggy mop of hair hung over his eyes.

"Too bad." Rutger shrugged a shoulder. "I had a good joke this time. You want to hear it anyway?"

"You can save it for next time," I said. "Know anything about what happened?"

"More than most," Howard said. "As usual. GC hasn't bothered to ask us anything, though."

"What did you see?"

"Heard, first," Rutger said. "From the third floor. Doll screamed louder than usual. Like a person in shock, not the sex noises you normally hear coming from the tower. This one was real."

"Blood curdling," Howard added.

"So we took notice. Looked up at the tower, soon enough, this sexdoll opens a window, climbs out in her lingerie, sees our tent, jumps on it. Three floors. I thought they was programmed not to injure themselves. One of three fundamentals, or something."

"They are." Androids of any kind had that built into their programming. Of course, it could be overridden if a human commanded them to do otherwise. To hurt themselves. And there were plenty of sick Johns who frequented The Boneyard for that very reason. They'd have to pay repair costs, but still, it happened. What didn't happen was forcing a doll to jump out a window. Why would a person do that? Rent a room with a sexdoll and command it to jump out a window? That would be all kinds of twisted. And unlikely. More likely was the doll jumped out on her own volition. But that wouldn't make sense, either. Self harm, not to mention questionable motive. But she saw the tent.

"You think she tried to cushion her fall?"

"Absolutely," Howard said. "I could see it in her face. Or her mannerisms, rather. She didn't want to jump, but it was like she had to. Like she decided to. And she flung herself out and used our home like a trapeze net."

"Then what?"

"Then she goes running down the alley. We looked up at the window, but nobody else poked their head out. Not for a few minutes, at least. And that was Bone, checking on the situation."

"Thanks." I handed him a goola chip.

The secret door slid open along the building's back wall. Bone poked his head out. "Alan! Good, you came. Thanks, man."

I approached the opening in the wall. He was in a bathroom stall. To his left was a dingy toilet. Toilet paper was stuck to his shoes.

"Okay, so a sexdoll supposedly killed a John, which is impossible, and then jumped out the fucking window, which is impossible. What's the real story?"

"The real story is I'm screwed." His white mohawk was saturated with glow cream today, and the faint light gave his eyes a sunken, shadowed look. "They'll probably take my license for this. If they determine it was due to the ManiAc Virus."

"Manic Virus? That's harmless." I thought of Listic, and her hyperactive, non sequitur, unintentionally misinformative nature. "Annoying as heck maybe, but harmless."

"No, not MV. MAV. ManiAc Virus. It's a new strain, causes AI's to go batshit. Even kill."

I shook my head. "There is no such thing, Bone. Too many failsafes. A person can ask an AI to subdue a perceived threat, but not kill someone, let alone destroy itself. And an AI certainly can't decide to do any of those things on its own. There are no renegade replicants running around with chips on their shoulders."

"No renegade whatsis?"

"Nevermind." Sometimes I forgot not everyone shared a passion for old movies like I did. Hardly anyone watched movies anymore. "I'm just saying there are so many coding laws hardwired into AI cores, there's no way an android could kill a human. Hasn't happened for a hundred years. It's basic, binary DNA."

"Yeah, Alan. I know about the fucking Robot Wars of Jupiter, I took the same general ed courses everyone else did. We all know about World War IV and the subsequent creation of the Artificial Intelligence Code. But tell that to the John upstairs. You know she tore his—"

"Yeah, I heard."

"The AIC still doesn't keep hackers from hacking. I mean, look at your ORB. Listic's a mess. Oh, that reminds me, I know I've been remiss in getting that antivirus to you. Things have been crazy at The 'Yard, right?"

"Sure."

"Like I need cops outside my restroom waiting for me to flush."

"Uh huh."

"Not that they can hear anything. Room's scrambled. Anyways..." He sounded overwhelmed.

"So what are you hoping I can do?"

"Okay, here it is: Find the doll. Before they do. If they find her, they'll dismantle her. And she's my top model, Alan. I'd lose a killing of goola if I don't get her back." He pulled a flier out of his back pocket and hands it to me. An advertisement brochure, showcasing the two dozen or so sexdolls that worked at his establishment. "I circled her. Name's Gwen. But it wasn't the doll, right? It was the ORB the client brought in. I'd swear on it."

I thumbed through his brochure, looking for the circled model. Most of the dolls were females ranging from elegant looking call girls to trashy hookers. There were men, too, ranging from beefcakes to playboys. There were women with men parts, and men with women parts. Some had fur, or horns, or tails, or green skin, or blue skin. The range was astonishing. Finally I found the one he circled. Gwen. Even I had to admit she was beautiful, and dolls weren't my thing. Short brown hair, dark brown eyes, olive skin, small hoop earrings, blue jeans and a tank top. She lacked the industry standard tattoos. She looked genuine, approachable. The girl next door.

"So the John brought his own ORB, jacked it into her eye socket?"

"Yeah. We inventory our clients. Before they rent a room, you know? He had an ORB on him. We didn't think anything of it, happens all the time. Figured it was loaded with a kinky template of some kind, or his ex-girlfriend's personality matrix, or something. You know how it goes."

"Sure."

"Only this is what I think. I think it was loaded with the ManiAc Virus. And I think it was loaded by Flickers."

"Flickers? The real-girl brothel on the other side of town?"

"Absolutely, man! They've been trying to shut me down for years. Business. They've been going for that 'unsafe' angle on my joint in the media. Trying to convince people they can get hurt by coming here."

A heavy knocking landed on the restroom door behind him. Thanks to the room's scrambler, we could hear them, but they couldn't hear us. "Hey Bone, you done in there? We still have questions." I recognized the voice. Conner. Which probably meant Lexi was on the other side of that door, as well. Young GalactiCops out to prove themselves. Too new to comprehend the subtle art of favor-trading. They'd be tough to shake.

"Hold your panties, I'm coming!" he replied to no one. "Gotta go. So that's the deal, Alan. I am being conspired against by Flickers, and I need you to get my doll back and prove my theory."

"Assuming I even think your theory is credible. So many unlikelies, Bone..."

"Please, Alan. It's not like the GC is going to credit my idea. I need you to do this for me. Or I'll maybe go out of business. I'd rather Flickers go out of business."

I sighed. "I'll see what I can do."

"Thanks, Alan. I owe you one." He turned off the scrambler, flushed the toilet, and slid the secret door shut.

Howard cleared his throat behind me. I turned to look at him, and he gave me the sign to skedaddle. Someone was coming. I lunged behind the only wall of their tent that was still upright, peaked out through a hole in its canvas.

"Knock knock," Rutger said to two approaching GalactiCops.

"Who's there?" one of them volunteered.

"Ibet Yor."

"Ibet Yor who?"

"Ibet Yor hoping for a gonut, but all you got was this fucking knock knock joke."

The second cop chuckled.

"Alright, wise guys," the first one said. "We've got a few questions for you."

"We love questions!" Howard said. I heard him slide his goola bowl toward them. "Almost as much as we love eating."

I slunk away in a crouch, keeping out of view. My involvement in this mess would need to be less public in nature. Fuck if I didn't step in a wad of gum on my way out of the alley.

3

Coffee Break

So I needed to find a crazy sexdoll. Where to start? Perhaps with a little crazy of my own.

I took my ORB out of my pocket and tossed her into the air. "Listic, On."

She lit up blue. "What's up, boss?"

"This is who we're looking for." I showed her Gwen's picture, pointed back a few buildings at The Boneyard. It was dark out, but I knew she could see with her enhanced night vision optic. "Jumped out of that window, landed on that tent, ran in this direction. Anything you can use to track her?"

"Hmmm... Maybe." She floated over to a little man sitting on a shuttle-stop bench, legs dangling, and projected an image of the photograph above his lap. "Excuse me, kind sir. Have you seen this sexdoll?"

"Say what?"

"Have you seen this sexdoll?" Listic cleared her nonexistent throat. "I don't mean 'seen her' seen her, I just mean seen her. Know what I mean?"

"No, I have not seen her, nor have I 'seen her' seen

her, and frankly I don't see what business it is of yours if I—"

"Alright, that's enough Listic." I caught up with her and palmed her. "Leave the nice man alone."

"You gotta keep that thing on a leash," he told me.

"You oughta be on a leash!" Listic muffled back. I didn't reprimand her for that one. Merely walked back toward the corner building, Bail Bond Breakers—the sign for which was flat against its wall, I might add— and opened my hand so she could float again. "You believe that guy?"

"I was hoping for something a little more forensic in nature."

Listic's iris brightened. "Oooooooohhh," she sang, as though I'd let her in on some kind of secret. "Well why didn't you saaaaay so." She zipped back down the alley behind The Boneyard, bounced around near the window and the tent and chatted it up with the GC's standard-variety ORB that was doing essentially the same thing. I caught her POV on my wristscreen— another piece of old tech from Remy's Gizmo's and Gadgets Galore, thanks to my increase in case revenue. Now I could see what Listic saw in real time, as well as playback her recordings. I had to tell her to record ahead of time, though. She didn't record anything by default. In any case, the device made most cheating spouse cases a cakewalk. It was almost too easy.

I was fortunate to be able to afford such a toy these days. I always found it curious how success could bring about success. The more you had, the more you could spare, and the more you could spare, the more you could gain. Conversely, if you couldn't spare a single goola chip, you couldn't invest in anything. In fact, it was all the easier to fall apart in a time of crisis. To hit rock bottom. Social momentum, either way.

People claim to have control over their lives, but I honestly think we're more victims to circumstance than we like to believe. Did Rutger and Howard choose to be homeless? Or did something happen to them, some piece of bad luck, that tipped their momentum in that direction, and now they're telling knock knock jokes for goola? Why does anyone do what they do? Because they choose to, sure. But they choose what they choose because of what's happened to them, and what's happened to them was often out of their hands. For the most part, for most people, life is nothing but a bunch of lucky breaks or unintended consequences.

"What on Fillion are you thinking about?" My nose appeared on my wristscreen, an extreme close up that informed me of grooming negligence. I looked up and saw Listic three inches from my face.

"I'm not even sure."

"You looked like you were immersed in some kind of tangential thought nugget regarding the meaning of life."

"My usual, then. So you find anything?"

"Perfume. The kind that make humans horny. Very trackable."

"Perfect."

"Also, gotta say, wow, what an incompetent ORB. The one the GC's are using, TXT-179, has no idea what he's doing. I told him to look for fingerprints, and he's probably still at it. Like dolls have fingerprints, Alan."

"It believed you? You can convince each other to do things? One ORB to another?"

"Well, sure. Why not?"

"I thought... I mean..." There was no way to say it without being blunt. "You're an artificial intelligence."

"No, you're an artificial intelligence, Alan." She sniffed with a nonexistent nose. "And you should be on a leash!"

"Okay, look. I'm sorry." Jesus, I was apologizing to a floating eyeball. "Let's move on. You say you picked up some perfume?"

"Boy, did I. That doll was caked in libido. I can track her down anywhere. Unless she headed out to the terraformer plant near the dome's base, of course. Too many olfactory signatures over there to distinguish one from another."

She turned away and floated with purpose. I followed my bouncy ball down the street and deeper into the night.

· ● ·

An hour later, we ended up at the terraformer plant near the dome's base.

"Well, shit."

Listic darted around the area, but this only served to exacerbate her artificial anxiety. "Yep. Lost the trail. What do we do now, boss?"

We'd travelled on foot well beyond the downtown area, even walked through the up and coming Fillion Edgeworld University's campus with all its lofty architecture, to reach this subsequent industrial wasteland. The terraformer plant itself was a huge collection of towers and shafts and cogs and pulleys, all rusted and corroded and straining against their own parts. This one was one of the older plants—not all of them had been replaced, yet—and it was always breaking down. Locals nicknamed it London. Steam emitted from a couple machines at such a rate as to create a dense fog bank. Not only was it impossible for Listic to smell anything, it was next to impossible for me to see anything. Beyond ten feet, anyway.

Much like leaping from the window to the tent, running out here connoted self-preservation. And intelligence. An intelligence not unlike the kind Listic herself developed after acquiring the Manic Virus—the thing that set her apart from the generic TXT models, the thing that caused me to get into arguments with her. Maybe this android was hacked, after all. Or the ORB the John put in her, at least. Maybe Bone was right, and there was such a thing as the ManiAc Virus.

I suddenly didn't feel as secure without my pistol and vibroknuckles. Having started this whole night on a cheating spouse case, I hadn't bothered to weapon up. I wasn't about to poke around unarmed in a steam bath. Besides, she probably wasn't even in there, anymore. Could have exited from a different point along the perimeter. This was a dead end.

Rule #7 of being a good private detective: When faced with a dead end, turn the fuck around.

"I'll head back to my office, grab my knuckles, gun, and face mask. Hop on the hoverbike and scope out the area at a quicker clip. If she wandered back out, maybe you can pick up her trail again."

"Okie dokie."

I turned around and headed back toward town. Since we were no longer following perfume, I cut a more direct path that didn't involve trekking through the university campus, hoping to save some time. This of course meant I only made things more complicated. I'd never gone this way before, and I didn't realize there was a natural ravine between here and the city. The ravine stretched off to the right for who knows how far, meaning if I doubled back, I'd erase most of the progress I'd made. It made more sense to go down and up again.

I recalled my recent exchange with Alice, about the wall of death. And I wondered if all this time, since the Academy, if I hadn't actually needed to climb up and over such obstructions on a regular basis, or if I simply hadn't noticed it. Like after I moved the couch up the flight of stairs to my new office, I found myself noticing other flights of stairs—how they were arranged, and how difficult it would be to move a couch up them. "Now that flight of stairs would suck," I'd say to myself. "All those angles. You'd really have to pivot on that intermediate landing." Or like when you learned a new word, the way you suddenly heard it everywhere, like three more times that week. You couldn't help but wonder if that word was always being said that frequently and you simply hadn't noticed it before, or if the word was suddenly in vogue.

All I knew was, I hoped climbing walls wasn't suddenly in vogue.

It was nearly 1 a.m. by the time Listic and I made it back to my office. The brownstone facade, catching a warm glow from the streetlamp, was a welcome sight. The ravine had killed my staying power. It was true what Alice said about life after the Academy: No one forced you to exercise in the real world, and you could eat all the crackdogs you wanted. A dangerous combination. Note to self: Use your goddamn exercise equipment, Alan!

I felt like I needed more than a regular night's sleep; I needed to go comatose. Hell, I needed to rent one of those forgone cryopod containers for a month. Even Listic acted tired. Her iris had dimmed. Probably in power-save mode.

"Oh, thank god," I said as my office came into view.

"Can't wait to curl up in my auxiliary charging cradle."

"I might sleep on the office couch. Not worth biking to the apartment at this hour. We can hunt down the doll first thing in the morning."

"First thing in the morning."

I unlocked the ground level door I shared with The Chicken Shack. Didn't bother to flip on the light in the stairwell. Climbed the creaky steps up to the second floor. Unlocked my office door. Realized I didn't need to.

My door latch was busted. Someone had broken in.

"C'mon, Alan" Listic whined. "What's the hold up? I'm down to one bar."

"Shhhh..." I held a finger to my lips and pointed at the door latch with my other hand.

Listic looked down at it. "Oh, snap."

I imagined whoever was in there, if they were still in fact in there, was sniffing around at my desk, and my desk was the first thing a person would encounter upon entering the room. The couch was off to the left side of the room, buffered by a low coffee table, and there'd be no reason for an intruder to muck around over there. The closet was off to the right. They might be in the closet. I'd have to be prepared for that. Knock open the door, aim to tackle a desk sniffer, but be ready to defend myself if someone came at me from the closet.

Or I could turn around. And call the GalactiCops. And call attention to my investigation. No thanks. Besides, I'd had enough hiding today. Late night stakeouts, back alley slink-aways, dysfunctional fog banks... I was anxious to finally catch someone. Anyone.

I stepped back from the entrance as far as I could, braced myself against the bannister railing, and flung myself through the door at full throttle. It swung open more easily than I'd expected, its latch being broken, and I went headlong past the faux leather guest chair and slammed into my desk.

I should reiterate how exhausted I was at this point. All the same, when nobody's available to tackle, and tackling is on your agenda, you kind of set yourself up to be an ass. It's like lifting a five-gallon jug of water only to discover there's no water inside. Tackling nobody feels kind of like that.

I recovered, shuffled my feet and stood up, fists cocked, waiting to take down whatever came at me from my closet.

"Why on Mother Earth would you do that?" said a woman's voice to my left. Confident. Intelligent. Nonthreatening. "You are Alan Blades, right? Isn't this your own office?"

I turned around sheepishly, fists still cocked, feeling like a dipshit. And there she was, sitting upright on my couch, wearing nothing more than black lingerie beneath a ripped and ratty trench coat. Steam rose from my favorite brown mug on the coffee table in front of her.

I recognized the trench coat as one of Rutger's. She must have grabbed it from their tent before tearing out of the alley.

"Gwen."

She rolled her eyes and brushed her hands through a mess of thick brown hair, then leaned forward. "Yeah, let's start with that. My name's not Gwen. My name's Rebeka Sterngard. I'm an extraterrestrial anthropologist who woke up while I was being used by a sicko in a sex chamber. I have no idea how I got there, and I have no idea how my body turned into... this."

"I think I need to recharge, Alan," Listic said. "Because none of that made any sense."

"You're a private detective, right? You won't report me to the authorities? You won't turn me in if I hire you?"

"Hire me to do what?"

"To protect me. To help me figure out how I got here. To help me figure out who—this!—is." She hit her own chest three times. "Mr. Blades, you have to help me. I've got nowhere else to go."

4

Friendly Visit

So much for sleep.

I'd made myself a cup of coffee and offered her another. Not that she needed it. She was an android. Maybe. But even though they renewed their energy by plugging into a wall overnight, they were designed to fake eat and drink with their clients as requested. It was a matter of being social, and sharing a meal with someone was arguably more intimate than sex. She'd already rifled through my stuff and made her own cup of coffee, but even so, she took me up on the offer. Said it was the blandest coffee she'd ever tasted, but it helped calm her nerves—the simple act of drinking it, holding it in her hands. The habit.

This was no artificial intelligence. It couldn't have been. If it was, it was loaded with more trivial detail than anything I'd encountered before. Hers wasn't a personality meant solely for the purpose of pleasing a client within an hour. But god help me if when I looked into her eyes there wasn't a person in there. I was usually quite capable of distinguishing a real person from an android. That's why I never took Bone's sexdolls up on any of their solicitations. They weren't real enough for me.

But this Rebeka Sterngard couldn't possibly be an android. No AI was that convincing, that vulnerable. Because that's an attribute that makes humans human. Vulnerability. And when this doll poured the half and half into her mug, her hands were shaking, and a drop or two didn't make it in the cup.

Something was up. I just didn't know what.

I had put my desk trashcan in front of my busted office door to keep it closed, dragged my client chair over to sit opposite the coffee table, and allowed her to hold her claim on the couch.

"So, Dr. Sterngard—"

"Bek. You can call me Bek."

"Bek. Let's start with how you ended up in my office. Guide me to this moment."

"Well, that much I remember. I remember everything since defending myself from that asshole. When I woke up in there, I was disoriented. And freezing. God, I was so cold. And this guy, he was making me… I don't want to talk about what he was making me do. How badly did I hurt him, anyway?"

"You hurt him all the way. He's dead."

"Oh my god." She put her hands up to her mouth. Genuine shock. "I didn't mean to… I was only trying to defend myself. To get out of there. I killed him?"

"I'm afraid so."

She sat there a moment, trying to get her bearings. Went for her coffee, took another sip, put the mug back on the table. "None of this makes any sense! I'm not that strong. There's no way I could have killed him."

"I hate to remind you of this, but that's an android body you're... in. Lack of strength is an imposition of regulators. Meaning dolls are normally weaker, but only because their throttles are closed. If the overrides are removed, if the throttles are opened, they essentially have super strength."

"I do feel... stronger. I was too freaked out to realize how strong I was back in the room. But after I jumped out the window, ran until I reached the edge of this crappy city, I picked up on how fast I was going. And how far I was going. And I wasn't even tired. I saw that fog out there in the distance, kept running toward it. Right into a fucking wall. That's when I discovered I must be in a dome city, and I was running around in a terraform plant. Well, I wasn't about to stay out there. I mean, what would the point of that be? So I crept back into town. What planet is this, anyway?"

"Fillion."

"The name sounds vaguely familiar... But no, I don't think I've heard of it."

"A lot of people haven't. Well, until recently. It's still thought of as an Edgeworld, despite its recent incorporation into the Victorian Cluster." She looked at me like I was speaking a foreign language. Was she that unaware of intragalactic news? I figured even people in The Core had heard about the newly established Victorian Cluster. "But that's a whole other story. So you crept back into town..."

"Yes. And I saw the GalactiCop precinct from a distance, but I didn't want to go there. I had no idea what was going on, so I wouldn't have even known what to tell them. I'd sound insane. If anything, after what happened in that room, I figured they might even lock me up. But I was thinking maybe I should do that—turn myself over to them, try to explain myself, and roll with it. Until I saw your sign out front."

"It's a good sign, isn't it?"

"I mean, I guess so."

"As far as signs go."

"It's... functional."

"Thanks, I'll take that. So you saw the sign out front—"

"And broke in. Yes. The bottom door was unlocked, but I had to break into your office. I'm sorry about that, by the way. I'll pay for the damage."

I glanced back at the door. "You are strong, alright. The only other woman I knew with that kind of strength was my ex-partner. And that wasn't until the ex part. She'd gotten a whole package of state of the art—"

Cybernetic components. And that's when it hit me. This woman wasn't an android. She wasn't riding an ORB's tweaked AI. There was no Manic Virus, no ManiAc Virus, no virus of any kind causing her to behave this way. She was indeed a person. She was a cyborg. Like Gina, my ex-partner. Inside that head of hers must have been the organic matter that gave humans their humanity. Nothing less than a brain.

That was the only thing that made sense.

But if that were the case, wouldn't she know this herself? Wouldn't she know she was a cyborg? And how would she have ended up at The Boneyard?

"'A whole package of state of the art' what?"

"Sorry?"

"You were saying? About your ex-partner."

"Oh. Yeah, ah…" I scratched my chin. I may have already told her too much. I hadn't agreed to take her on as a client yet, and if she was lying to me about all this, or any of this, whether she was a cyborg or not, I could end up going down a rabbit hole that would get me into a lot of trouble. I'd be breaking one of my cardinal detective rules. Rule #2: Keep what you know to yourself.

But then there was my fundamental rule. The rule that trumped all the others. Rule #1: Always trust your gut.

And my gut told me, for some inexplicable reason, I could trust this woman.

"I was saying she was a cyborg. Or she became one. It was still her, but her body had been enhanced. Cybernetics. You think, maybe…"

"That I'm a cyborg? I mean, sure. Who isn't, these days? Almost everyone's got an implant of some kind."

"Not so much, out here on the Edgeworlds. We use ORB's, for example, but most of us don't have implants, so they serve as peripheral devices."

I thumbed back at Listic, sleeping soundly in her cradle. Her blue iris glowed and faded, glowed and faded, while she recharged. The fact that Bek assumed we all had implants led me to believe she wasn't from around here. Probably from Orion, possibly The Core.

"So you guys walk around with floating eyeballs? That's weird."

"Not really."

"No, that's weird. Like, really weird."

"Whatever, we're used to it. So what implants do you have?"

"The eye one, obviously. The interface, so I can actually plug my ORB in and use its standard optic features. And... This is embarrassing, but my husband and I—I mean, my ex-husband and I—we splurged on that new feature. The IA."

"You mean an AI? That's nothing new. Heck, even Listic's got an AI. It's a basic feature."

"No, not an AI. An IA. Intimate Ansible. It allowed Hank—that's my ex-husband—it allowed us to communicate with each other wherever we went. Closed network, only the two of us—which was obviously more limiting than the omniquark ansible network— but always on, always synced. That was supposedly its 'asset.'"

"I thought they outlawed those. Like, thirty years ago."

"What? No, that isn't possible. I mean, I can see why they'd be outlawed, they're a horrible fucking idea. No off button? You receive each other's feeds wether you like it or not. Let me tell you, there is such a thing as too intimate. But I mean, they're new. They just came out. At least, that's what the rep told us. It was super expensive, but we got a discount, on account of signing up for their pilot program. That was part of why we couldn't turn it the fuck off, we were locked into this contract that..."

My mind wandered into another train of thought while she went on about how horrible it was to spend every waking moment linked to her husband's most private moments. Things better left unknown, or in this case, left unexperienced. She thought this was new technology? If she had such easy access to cybernetic implants, she must have grown up closer to The Core. But if that were the case, she would have known about the whole IA debacle. It was stellar legend. No way she could have been that out of touch, and no way both her and her husband could have been duped into signing up for such a proven disaster.

I had been focusing on the wrong half of the space-time continuum. It wasn't a matter of where. It was a matter of when.

"...Not to mention, he had a wandering eye, if you know what I mean. If he noticed another woman, I'd notice her, too. Even after the divorce, it was still annoying. I mean, I know he's a guy, I get it, but still. Are all men like that? It was almost like he had a built in radar for—"

"Bek?"

"What."

I cleared my throat. "What year do you think it is?"

"Core Calendar?"

"Core Calendar."

"2145."

"Bek?" I pursed my lips.

"It's 2145, right? October something?"

"Bek, it's 2278."

"What! You're lying. You have to be lying..."

"I'm sorry, but it is. You can check the feeds. It's August 23, 2278 CC."

I went over to my desk and grabbed my holopad, then brought it back to the couch and set it on the coffee table. I opened the newsfeed. A page emitted above the pad. The top story headline read "Killer Sexdoll on the Loose! Boneyard Patron Dead at the Scene!" But that wasn't news to Bek. What was news was the date at the top: 8/23/2278.

"No. No, no, no, no... This can't be right." She flicked through the feed. Article after article, interspersed by ads from Dan's Genetically Modified Steak House, all held the same date. "I lost... a hundred and thirty years?" She turned the holopad off and looked across my office with an empty stare. "Although... that would explain something."

"And what would that be?"

"Why I haven't experienced anything from Hank since I... since I woke up in that room." She plopped back into the couch cushions with resignation. "The asshole's dead."

"I'm sorry. This has got to be hard to absorb."

She nodded slowly. Even if their marriage didn't work out, they were still connected. That had to be a powerful loss. Hell, even after my marriage didn't work out with Margo, I still shared a past with her. Still even kept in touch. It wasn't all bad. When you're that close to someone for that long, they become a part of you. And in Bek's case, even more so.

Her eyes teared up a little. Android tears? She wiped at them.

"Tell me the last thing you remember."

"Running. Running from..." She didn't finish.

"Running from..."

"I don't think I'm ready to talk about that yet. It depends."

"On what?"

"Listen, are you taking my case, or not?"

I had to stop and think a moment. If I took her on, I'd be sworn to secrecy. Client confidentiality. If I told the authorities anything—any authorities—I could have my private detective license revoked. And I didn't know enough about her situation to guarantee I wouldn't have to disclose something she told me, at some point, to someone else. There were still far too many unknowns. For starters, I didn't even have proof she was a cyborg rather than an android. I was going on my gut. A lot of it hinged on that. If only I had a means of distinguishing that factor. Where was a good Turing Test when you needed one?

Bek sat there, looking at me expectantly. I sat there, staring at the coffee table. In the silence, I could hear the hum of Listic's cradle.

Of course! Listic! I'd used her for this purpose before. All I needed to do was jack her into Bek. Listic could verify whether or not she was a cyborg.

"I'll take your case, but only under one condition," I said.

She brightened a little. "What's the condition? Besides, I'm the one who should be skeptical. How do I know you're any good? I mean, you don't even wear a fedora..."

"I'm plenty good, and I've been meaning to get a fedora. Hear me out." I looked over at my desk. "Listic, On."

She brightened and lifted an inch from her cradle. "Seriously, do you really need me right now? I'm only at

30%. You're waking me up during REM."

"Listic, do you remember how you determined Gina was a cyborg? Back on the Century Pigeon?"

"I'm groggy, Alan."

"Shake it off."

She vibrated. "Yes, I remember."

"Okay." I looked back at Bek. "Here's what I need you to do. It might feel a little strange, but I need to jack Listic into your eye socket. In order to confirm you're a—"

A heavy knock landed on my door. Fortunately, my trashcan was weighed down with enough of my junk to keep it from flying open. But the fact the door was still closed didn't keep the interruption from scaring the crap out of us. And the words that followed were even more nerve wracking.

"GalactiCops. We know you're in there, Blades. Open up."

· · ·

Time froze. Bek looked at me wide-eyed, then looked around at the couch. She pointed behind it and mouthed the words "Back here?" I shook my head. We'd have to scoot the couch away from the wall too far, it would be an obvious hiding spot. I pointed behind me and mouthed the word "Closet." She nodded and wormed her way around the coffee table, behind my desk, and into the closet.

"C'mon, Blades. Open up. Some of us have to sleep tonight."

"Hold your horse nuts, I'm coming."

I closed the closet door behind her and opened the office door two feet—narrow enough so it didn't look like I was inviting them in, but wide enough to where it didn't look like I was trying to hide anything.

"Yes, officers? Can I help you?"

It was Conner and Lexi, the ones who'd been questioning Bone. I knew these two, even had a relationship with them—if you can call antagonistic banter and noncommittal responses a relationship.

If there's one thing I didn't miss about being a GalactiCop, it was the outfits. Activated, they put Bone's glow cream to shame. Hell, they put the Hungry Pagoda's flaming dragon sign to shame. GC gear lit up like a flare gun on a dark night, red and blue suspenders flashing on and off, on and off. It was seizure inducing. And those oversize belts were nothing short of obnoxious. There really wasn't a need for them to be so wide, other than to call attention to their sidearm and intimidate the hell out of people.

"Hey look, Conner!" Lexi said. "He's willing to help us for a change! See, I told you he'd be willing to help us."

"So we're playing the chummy pal game today?" Conner asked me.

"Isn't 'chummy pal' redundant?" I asked.

"Fine, then." Lexi looked over to her partner. "Looks like it's another round of sarcastic asshole."

I stared at them with my "let's get on with it" stare.

"You were witnessed near the scene of a crime earlier," Conner said.

"What scene and what crime," I said.

"You know what scene, you know what crime. The Boneyard, Blades. A few hours ago. You know the proprietor, Henry 'Bone' DeWalsch. Do cases for him, get information from him. You two have a connection."

"You know I'm a private detective, right? This means I go about detecting things. Privately. That's kind of how it works. Since when is doing my job a crime?"

"Since maybe a few hours ago," Lexi interjected. "We have reason to believe you were fed information by him he neglected to tell us. Regarding a psychotic sexdoll. And the withholding of that information, should you refuse to tell us after being asked, would amount to impeding an investigation and obstructing justice. And guess what? We're asking."

I shrugged my shoulders. "Did you see me there?" I looked back and forth between the two of them. "Either of you? Any of you?"

"We don't need to disclose who saw you, only that we have reason to believe you were there."

"Well I have reason to believe you don't have any credible evidence to substantiate your claims, and I am not about to voluntarily disclose any information I don't even have. I know how this works too, you know."

A thunk came from my closet, and a muffled voice said "Shit!"

"Who was that?" Conner asked, tiptoeing to look over my shoulder.

"Oh, that's my ORB," I said. "Manic Virus, with a touch of Turrets. Cusses up a storm for no reason, sometimes."

Listic's intuition chip kicked in to save my ass. She

rocketed around the room with a potty mouth. "Shit fuck mother fucker!" she screamed. "Ass wipe!"

"She can be a real pain."

"Uh huh," Lexi said. She was not sold. "Let us in, Alan."

"Show me your warrant, Lexi."

"Oh, we can get a warrant." She brushed her short black bangs to the right and smiled.

"A warrant to search a private detective's office for, plausibly, being near the scene of a crime? I sincerely doubt it."

Conner looked as his watch. "C'mon, Lex, let's go. We'll come back tomorrow. Gotta check in on the murdered chauffeur incident."

"Wait, someone murdered a chauffeur?" I asked. "Does that have anything to do with this?"

"We may never know."

"Last chance, Alan," Lexi said. The games were over, and her look was honest. "You can do the right thing and help us. Or you can be part of the problem and allow a psychotic sexdoll to go on a killing spree."

"See you tomorrow," I said. The hallway looked like a disco party as they walked down the stairs in flashing suspenders. I closed my door and braced the trashcan in front of it again. "Always fun with those two."

I opened the closet door and saw Bek curled up in the corner. "So you believe me?"

I did. I didn't know why I did, but I did. "I still need you to do that thing I was going to have you do with my ORB. Mostly so we can figure out what to do next. But not here. We have to get out of here."

I peeked out my window blinds and watched Conner and Lexi having a conversation, or an altercation, on the sidewalk by their parked hovercar. Lexi was gesturing up toward my office with exasperation, Conner was shaking his head and put his hand on her shoulder to calm her down. I got the vibe they were not only partners, they were "partners," and their disagreement went beyond debating their jurisdiction in this manner. They might be at it for awhile.

Fortunately, my hoverbike was parked out back. And I had an alternate exit.

I reached my arm out to Bek and helped her up. My backup shirts and slacks draped over her shoulders as she stepped out of the closet. "Hey, you want to put on some of my clothes or something? You can't be comfortable running around in your underwear."

"I tried them on, already. Before you got here. They don't exactly fit this body. I've got curves where I didn't know curves were possible."

"Right," I looked her up and down quickly. Which caused my cheeks to flush.

She shook her head and said "Men" under her breath.

"Hey, you brought your curves up, where was I supposed to look, down at the floor?"

"I don't know. Maybe." She sighed. "I'm sorry, okay? I'm a little self-conscious right now. My real body isn't exactly shaped like this."

"No, I'm sorry. You're right. Men." I reached back into the closet, dug around behind my auxiliary wardrobe, and grabbed a long pole with a hook on it.

"Why do you have that thing, anyway?" She asked. "It fell on me."

"We heard."

"What, is it like a harpoon, or a javelin, or..."

I latched it onto a bar next to a hatch in the ceiling and pulled down a ladder. "I call it my 'hook on a stick.'" I rifled through my desk drawer and grabbed my vibroknuckles and my holstered sidearm, then grabbed my face mask from the wall mount. "Okay, I think I've got everything."

"Please tell me we won't need that."

"I mean, the air quality's been better lately, but I can't promise anything."

Listic aimed her optic at me. "I think she meant your sidearm, Alan."

"I did. I meant your sidearm."

"Oh. I thought you were talking about my face mask."

Listic hovered over to Bek and whispered. "He's not very bright sometimes."

"In my defense, I'm low on sleep." I took off my jacket and wrapped the weapon's holster around my chest, took the pistol out and checked its ammo, re-holstered it and put my jacket back on. "Trust me, I hope we won't need this, either."

I climbed up first and looked around. Listic rose to the occasion and met me at my shoulder. No one on the roof, but I could still see red and blue lighting up the street below.

She made the climb. I gathered up the ladder and closed the hatch, then guided her to another ladder mounted on the backside of the building, where my Honda was parked in the alley below. Another back alley. What was it about being in a back alley that made you feel like you were on the wrong side of things?

We climbed down and mounted my hoverbike. Listic dropped into her cradle on the dashboard, snapping into it like a magnet, and started charging the remaining two-thirds of her battery. Bek put on my spare helmet and became a bike warrior clad in lingerie and a trench coat.

She wrapped her arms around me from behind. "So where are we going?"

I ignited the engine and we floated on air jets. "My apartment complex."

"Don't you think that's the last place we should go?"

"Trust me, it's the safest place we can be." I lowered my helmet's visor. "No one fucks with my landlady."

5

Movie Night

I parked my bike along the side of my apartment complex and threw a tarp over it. Marple, my nefarious old landlady, was grabbing a smoke in front of her own apartment at the far end of the first floor. I gave her a short, brisk wave after directing Bek upstairs to my second floor abode. Marple replied in kind with her cigarette before flicking the ash off it. It was more than an exchange of hellos; it was a sign of solidarity. Don't pay your rent on time, and Marple was a force to be reckoned with, a five-foot, seventy-five-year-old package of eviction incarnate. But keep your end of the bargain on the first of every month, and you had yourself the planet's best doorwoman. Marple put Bone's bouncers to shame.

Bek was scrutinizing the entryway of my place, with its peeling plaster and exposed brick, as I came up behind her with my door key. She reached out and touched part of the wall that needed some patching up.

"It's not much to look at, I know. But it's got walls and a roof, and as long as you don't decide to bust it open with your super-strength, a door that actually latches."

"Oh no, I wasn't judging. Just reflecting on the cultural and physical construct of home. There are so many versions of what amounts to a home. Some are siloed, others are shared. And then there are mixtures of the two, like this apartment complex, where people live right next to each other, yet lead entirely separate lives. It's the anthropologist in me I guess, always thinking about how people interact with each other."

I scooted past her to reach my door. "I can't say I ever gave it much thought."

"I grew up in an apartment complex like this. Even though my father did his best to shelter me, I found myself conversing with all my neighbors. Dale was the best. Made dynamite grockjuice. You know your neighbors well?"

"I know Rickshaw's an asshole. He lives downstairs."

I unlocked my door and went in. Listic floated past me and sank into her primary charging cradle without saying a word. She settled in, but didn't power down entirely.

I tugged the light switch on the floor lamp and exposed my bachelor pad in all its slovenly glory. My place was a mess. But I hadn't realized it until now. It's amazing how that worked, how you rarely acknowledged your clutter, dust, and carpet stains until you had a guest over. I hadn't taken the trash out for a few days, and I'd let the dishes go equally as long. My collection of physical data units were all over the living room—discs, cartridges, flash drives, many of them sporting reproductions of their original packaging, stacked on shelves, tables, and floor. In fact, the movie cases and dust jackets that enticed me to collect them now seemed garish and immature. I felt the need to explain myself. To a sentient sexdoll. Or a cybernetic anthropologist. Or whatever.

"Oh my god," Bek said.

"Yeah, I know. Sorry, it's a mess. I haven't put much effort into keeping it tidy, now that my place no longer doubles as my office. I thought I'd end up with more space, you know? Like that would kind of open it up. But I ended up putting an exercise machine over there where my desk used to be, not that I ever use it, and—"

"Oh. My. God."

"Okay, seriously? It's not that bad, is it?"

Bek tore past me and grabbed a DVD from the eye-level shelf of my shallow wooden bookcase. "You own Raiders of the Lost Ark?" She looked over at me with an earnest enthusiasm only humans could convey. The more I interacted with her, the more I was convinced: Bek was no android.

"You know movies?"

"Yeah, I know movies!" she gushed. "Like I said, my dad, he tried to shelter me. And he came close to pulling it off, too, by getting me hooked on these things. He was a little eccentric, never up with the times. Never let me go to the holovids, never let me dip into VR. I used to resent him for it, especially when I was a teenager. But now I see it as a blessing. My god, I love this movie. No joke, it shaped my life. Set me on the course to extraterrestrial anthropology."

"Don't watch the fourth one," Listic said. "It's got aliens in it."

"Kingdom of the Crystal Skull?" she replied. "What do you mean, that's the best one!"

Neither Listic nor I said anything. What was there to say? This was devastating. Any feelings I was developing for Bek, whether I'd wanted to admit to them or not, went flying out the airlock. She liked Crystal Skull. This was enough to make me question her humanity all over again. In fact, it gave credence to Bone's theory that she'd acquired the ManiAc Virus. Arguable insanity.

It was probably for the best, though—not having feelings for her. She was a client, after all. Wouldn't want to complicate matters...

"Got ya!" Bek said, crouching and pointing a finger at me. "The look on your face!" She laughed. "Priceless!"

"Oh, thank god," Listic said. "Thank god, Alan."

I clutched my chest and let out a long breath. "You really—heh—had me—heh heh—had me, there."

Bek was laughing so hard, it was contagious. "And your ORB!" she screamed. "Whatsername! She just—tahimf!—stared at me!" She plopped onto the couch holding her stomach. I had to sit down, as well. The more she laughed, the more I did.

Eventually we caught our breath regained our composure. She leaned back into the corner of the couch. I had to admit, she looked rather enticing in that outfit—or lack thereof. But what I was most attracted to was her personality. AI template or not, I'd never met someone like her before.

"Okay, Alan Blades," she asked in a low voice. "What are you going to do to me?"

"I—um, what?"

She leaned forward. "You said it might feel a little weird."

"I... I did?" I started to feel a little weird myself.

"Your ORB?" She nodded past me over to Listic. "You don't remember telling me that? Back at your office?"

"My ORB!" I let out a sigh of relief. "Of course! I need to put Listic in you. For a diagnostic. Yes, absolutely."

She looked perplexed. "Wait, what did you think I was talking about?"

"Nothing," I said. "Listic, float over here."

Bek took in a short breath. "Oh! Oh, I'm so sorry. I hope you didn't think I meant... I mean, I wasn't trying to suggest we... Well, we hardly know each other, and—"

Listic flew right between our faces. "Oh, for... Save it for the third act, you two!"

"Right." I reached out and grabbed Listic. "Okay, Bek. I need you to eject your ORB—the one the guy plugged into you at The Boneyard. Then you'll need to let me plug Listic into your eye cavity, instead. She can tell me if you're an android or a cyborg based on the interface. It might be a little unsettling, but it won't take long."

Bek took a deep breath. "And then what?"

I wasn't sure myself. "We'll dive into that subgate when we come to it."

We both sat there for a moment in silence. I gave her time to think. I needed her to be onboard with this.

"This is going to sound strange, but can we..." She looked at me and scrunched up her face. "Can we watch a movie, first?"

"What?"

"I need to watch a movie first. I know, totally weird. But this whole thing, it's... It's too much for me to handle, you know? I mean, I understand. I understand why you need to do this. I must sound like a mad woman. I can't imagine I'd believe me, either. But before I woke up in that room, I felt so..." She swallowed. I waited. "So isolated. And lonely. And cold! I'm not exactly anxious to fade back into a sense of... A sense of nothingness. I need to do something. Something normal, if only for a couple hours."

It was three a.m. To say I was exhausted would have been the biggest understatement of the twenty-third century. But I couldn't deny the earnest pleading of her voice. Sure, why not watch a movie with an as-yet-to-be-empirically-debunked murderous sexdoll at my side while on the verge of falling asleep?

Then again, there was my Rule #8 for being a good private detective: Always make time for movies.

"Okay," I said. "We'll watch a movie first."

"Yay!"

"Raiders of the Lost Ark?"

"I watched it for the dozenth time last week. Or a hundred and thirty years ago, give or take. No, not Raiders. But let's keep it in the Harrison Ford family. Do you have Star Wars?"

If this woman wasn't an android, I was in love.

I popped in Star Wars. Vintage DVD, original edition. For two hours, we geeked out over sappy dialogue and ancient special effects. Over three-hundred years later, the movie still had heart. Eventually, the Death

Star exploded, medals were awarded, and C-3PO got a wax job.

We let the credits roll for a bit. I was nodding off around Ron Tabera, Gaffer, but Bek jarred me awake.

"Okay, then." She nodded her head resolutely, took a deep breath, and sat up straight.

"Are you sure? You're ready?"

"If it means gaining your trust, absolutely. Let's do this." She took a deep breath, reached up to her face, and ejected her ORB. The loose eyeball fell to the couch and rolled into the crack between the green seat cushions. Bek sat perfectly still. Rigid, even.

"Bek?" I asked. I leaned forward and grabbed her upper arms. "Are you still there?"

The sexdoll snapped back to action, its remaining eye brown and glowing, but lifeless. I didn't even need Listic to confirm it. Bek had left the room.

"Name's Gwen, baby," the sexdoll said, reaching her arms around my neck and pulling in close. "But you can call me Bek, if you want to. You can call me anything."

6

Off Grid

Gwen's need to press her breasts in my face made it pretty obvious Bek was no longer in control, but I went ahead and inserted Listic, anyway. As a detective, I often had to go with my gut. But if the potential to prove something was readily available, I'd be a fool to pass it up. Gathering any and all evidence to reconstruct a scenario was as close as you could get to the scenario itself.

Although truth be told, piecing a crime together after the fact was more like approaching a value along logarithmic curve. The more evidence you could gather, the closer you'd get to the curve's limit. But you'd never reach the limit, never achieve a hundred percent certainty. You were always chasing a hundred percent, but you'd never get past ninety-nine and a decimal.

Even as witnesses, what we saw may not have been what we thought we saw. Memory plays tricks on us. The mind hates a data-void, so instead, it makes shit up. Fills in the blanks. Quite the irony, since we all walk around thinking we've got our act together, thinking we are the sum total of what we know. But when you stop and think about it, it's hard to "know" much of anything. Religious or not, most of life is faith-based. It's like we're never more than shadowing the truth. Kind of like that tree that falls in the forest. You have to assume the noise.

I popped my ORB companion into the android's head. Listic verified my assumption. No biological gray matter, no brain or mind or consciousness. No Bek.

Which could only mean Bek was in the eyeball. An Occipital Roaming Bot that didn't roam. As much as I hated to admit it, I'd fallen for an artificial intelligence. I was an easier target for Bone's sexdolls than I thought.

At that point, I probably should have turned the android in. The facts would show I was indeed harboring a psychodoll—albeit an extraordinarily genuine, movie-loving psychodoll—as the GalactiCops had surmised. I could technically remove myself from provable wrongdoing by claiming she was hiding in my office closet the whole time but I never knew: Sorry guys, here ya go, better late than never. They wouldn't believe me, and the scenario of hiding a sexdoll in my closet would give them enough material to make jokes at my expense for weeks, but they wouldn't press charges. Why waste the time?

After removing Listic, I switched "Gwen" off by flipping the power switch in her head socket. I moved her over to my bed, then took the opportunity to lay down on my couch. I suppose I could have left her on the couch and claimed the bed for myself, but something about that seemed rude, some remnant of chivalry from a bygone era still kicking around in my genes and applied to an inanimate—animate?—object. Anyway, I knew there were still things to do, but I couldn't help it. I needed to crash. I was flesh and blood, and I hadn't slept for nearly twenty-four hours.

I went as comatose as the doll for four solids, then woke up to an obnoxious alarm I had asked Listic to blare at the ripe hour of ten a.m. After chewing her out for the intrusion, she reminded me she was only doing what I'd asked her to do. I splashed some cold water on my face, then made my apologies.

I threw on a fresh shirt and asked Listic to keep an eye on the dormant android.

"Hah, very funny," she said, "because I'm an eyeball."

"I didn't mean it as a joke."

She lit up, already over it, on to the next thing. "Oh, hey! Why not let me interface with Gwen and mess around while you're gone?" She started floating toward the doll.

I put my hand out in front of her. "That will not be happening."

"Please, Alan? I promise I won't get too kinky."

"Too kink—what? No. Absolutely not." And then I thought of something that might clear up this whole mess: Listic couldn't interface with Bek the android, but maybe she could interface with Bek the ORB. "Actually, I need you to do something."

"What, you want me to set another alarm so you can yell at me some more?"

"I want you to communicate directly with Bek's ORB. The way you did with the GalactiCop ORBs in the alley behind The Boneyard." I held Bek's ORB in front of Listic. Eyeball to eyeball.

"Oh sure Alan. And then I'll go talk to a rock, because that'll be equally as stimulating."

"You mean..."

"There's nothing in there either, boss. No AI. No nothing."

Well, that didn't clear up shit. If Bek wasn't the android, and Bek wasn't the ORB, then who or what the hell was Bek?

I had to know. This was one of those cases where additional knowledge didn't bring you any closer to the logarithmic limit. It directed you away from it. I was less certain about what was going on now than ever. Nothing added up, and a part of me felt like if I turned the android over to the GC now, I'd be giving up on her. Not the Gwen part, but the Bek part.

Yet even though I wasn't willing to give up on her, I wasn't exactly ready to reactivate her, either. After all, it was upon awaking at The Boneyard when she killed a client. Would she be as dangerously disoriented this time around? I decided I'd do neither.

I slipped Bek's ORB into my pocket, left Listic in her cradle, and headed out. Gave Marple a nod and hopped on my hoverbike.

I knew a guy. Remy. He owned an old tech shop on the edge of town, and I was in there every week—most times to purchase movies, other times to replace the devices that actually played the movies. The devices were always breaking. But every now and again, I'd bring something to him so he could tell me what the hell it was. Maybe he could tell me what the deal was with this ORB.

I thought about possibilities as I rode my bike down vacant backroads. This ORB did look different, even I could tell that. Less refined, more... prototypical? I don't know, I was grasping at stardust.

A movie came to mind—one of the last ones ever produced, before they stopped making movies, entirely. Neuromancer, filmed in 2035, fifty years after the book it was based on was written, not to mention the very year the story supposedly took place. I'd only ever seen the movie, never read the book, but fans claimed it didn't do the book justice—although I suppose doing it justice would be impossible, given fifty years worth of expectations. Anyway, I recalled the plot being about an artificial AI developing a split-personality. Could that be what's going on? Maybe Bek's split off somehow? A hidden, partitioned personality?

I pulled my hoverbike into the dirt patch that served as Remy's parking lot, blowing up a cloud of dust as my bike's hover pads switched from antigravity to air-cushion for the comedown. The customer bell rang as I passed through the door. From the entrance, despite the piles and aisles of treasure and crap between me and the checkout counter, I caught a glimpse of Remy rifling through an opened shipping container with boyish glee. He was wearing that old tattered spaceball cap of his, its holographic Ruvellian Skybats logo projecting a few inches above its bill.

Remy loved unboxing shipments. He loved receiving new shit every day. What I couldn't fathom was the fact he also loved selling that very same shit every day. Like, how can you be so excited to acquire something, and then be as equally excited to let it go? Retail boggled my mind. I could never own a store like this, it would riddle me with separation anxiety.

I made my way to counter, past plastic and metal. Physical devices with buttons and switches, before the days of holopads and ethernet.

"Alan!"

"Remy."

"Hey, how's that wristscreen working out for you? You know, I got some great stuff in today. I don't think it's your kind of stuff, though. Mostly audio. You want to buy a walkman?"

"What's a walkman?" It sounded like something an invalid would use.

"They're these personal music-playing devices. Nineteen hundreds on Earth, then repopularized in the twenty-twos on Quartermast."

"I'll pass."

"Yeah, I know. Sorry, no movies, this round. And I still haven't come across any laserdisc players. But hey, weren't you in a couple days ago? You usually come by on Tuesdays..."

"I've got something I want you to check out." I pulled the ORB out of my pocket and handed it to him. He took it gently and twisted it around in his fingers while scrutinizing it with a furrowed brow. Everything was a collectible to Remy.

"I don't normally buy cyberwear, you know. But you're a pal. How much you want for it?"

"I'm not selling it. I'm trying to figure out what the hell it is."

"It's an ORB."

"Yeah, but what kind? There's something unusual about it."

"Is it busted? Or does it just need a charge..."

"No idea."

"You see it powered up before now?"

"I think so."

Remy looked back at the ORB and twisted it around some more. "You don't seem to know much about this thing, Alan."

"That's why I'm here."

"Hmmm..." He handed it back to me. "Sorry, I ain't much help. But the good news is, I know a guy."

I thought he would. Right in line with Rule #9 of being a good private detective: Know a guy who knows a guy.

"Who?"

"You heard of the Hack Shack?"

"Who hasn't heard of the Hack Shack? For that matter, who hasn't heard of Atlantis?"

"No, man. The Hack Shack? It's real."

"You're serious. Like, it's not a metaphor. It's an actual place."

Remy's expression turned sincere. "Yep. An actual, physical place."

"So where the hell is it? I've been up and down every beat of this city."

"It's outside the city. And it moves." He looked around for other customers, of which we both knew there were none, then leaned in closer to me and whispered. "Guy comes in two, three times a year. When my store's closed. Big guy. Needs a hover belt to stay upright, kinda makes him into this giant ballerina with cyberwear on his head. He's always trying to sell me this kind of stuff. Old cyberwear, the kind of stuff you normally only find vendors trading further out, toward the edge of the Edge. He gets his shit from that direction, whereas I get my shit from The Core. I tell him I'm not interested, but goddamn if he don't bring something legit in every third visit, something Core, like a Hyper Nintendo controller or an electric shaver. So I buy it, he keeps coming back. If this eyeball of yours is anything quirky, he'll know what it is, I guarantee it."

I put the ORB back in my jacket pocket. "Thanks, Remy. Appreciate it."

"Sure."

"So how do I find this guy?"

"Hmmm... You know, my memory might be a little fuzzy on that..." He pretended to think for a moment, then scooted that crazy audio contraption toward me. Wires and plastic and foam. "You sure you don't want a walkman? Requires double As, but I've got some on hand. They still make 'em—you know, for us weirdos. One customer, he said I should put 'em in the freezer to make 'em last longer. I figured it couldn't hurt.Hang on, I'll get 'em..."

I walked out of Remy's with a scuffed up walkman, a pair of cold batteries, and a broken cassette tape called Forever Your Girl by a Paula Abdul. I also walked out with directions to the Hack Shack.

· • ·

Listic was watching Star Wars when I got back. The volume was practically on mute—she didn't need it very loud for her super hearing to pick it up—but in my head I could still hear Luke whining about not getting to pick up more power converters.

Listic watched a lot of movies lately, even when I wasn't around. She couldn't change the discs or anything, but she'd use her infrared emitter as a universal remote and watch whatever happened to be in the player. I was sure it was mostly a result of the Manic Virus. That was one of the aspects of MV: It made an AI proactive rather than reactive. Empirically, at least. In actuality, it was a matter of binaries firing at random. Yet didn't that, along with memory, define human existence? Weren't people defined by proactive choices? By synapsis firing at random?

Even so, the Manic Virus didn't explain Listic entirely. What I didn't understand was why she needed to watch—or even more so, re-watch—movies in the real world rather than by playing them internally in her CPU. She had access to the Archives, after all. That's how she read Harry Potter so many times. It was as though she picked up yet another human trait every day. As though she was learning.

Was that what Bek was? An AI that caught a virus and learned how to impersonate a human realistically enough to ace the Turing Test? Some kind of adjustment that kicked in when a particular type of ORB was jacked in to her subset?

"Hi Alan," Listic said without rotating from the screen. She almost sounded like she was pouting.

I walked past her and grabbed my terrasuit from

the coat rack. I already had my sidearm and my vibroknuckles on me, those weren't what I'd come back for. I'd need my terrasuit for breaching the dome.

"Anything exciting happen while I was out?" I asked.

"Rebel spaceships, striking from a hidden base, have won their first victory against the evil Galactic—hey, are we going out?"

I folded my terrasuit into fourths and pinched it under my arm. "We are."

"Me too?"

"You too."

"Yes!" The television popped off. "Bek too?"

"Afraid not."

"Bummer," Listic looked over at her as she floated out the door with me. "I was beginning to like her."

Tempting as it was, I figured the android body was better off staying put. For all I knew, after Conner and Lexi had gotten over their squabble outside my office, they'd decided to stake out my place. I didn't much care if they tailed me making a regular trip to Remy's and back—that was standard Alan Blades behavior, and Remy knew how to keep his mouth shut—but if they saw me bring the doll out, it was all over. They'd take Bek off my hands and take her downtown for dismantling.

I figured if they tailed me I could lose them—this wasn't New Gaia, where the GC satellites could track your every move—but it would take a few blocks of sharp turns and double-backs, and I wasn't in the mood. Not yet, at least. I'd save the bike chase for later.

I locked my door behind me. Nothing but a slab of wood keeping Bek safe. Well, a slab of wood, and my increasingly limited right to privacy.

Marple was smoking a cigarette outside of her own place downstairs. "Your friend still in there, Alan?"

I nodded. "You know the drill."

She stood up straight and cocked her head, pretending to talk to someone a foot taller from a foot away, then shook her cigarette at his pretend face. "'Hey buddy. You gotta warrant?'"

"I wouldn't mess with you."

"Your lady friend could use some clothes. Send her my way when you get back."

"Thanks, Marple."

I headed down the stairs and stuffed my terrasuit into my bike's saddle bag. Hopped on. Put on my helmet.

"Hey," Marple added. "What if they have a warrant?"

"We're fucked." I ignited the engine.

"Well then," she said over the hum, "it's a good thing you're month to month!"

I waved and drove away.

. . .

No red and blue lit up behind me. I doubled back and forth a few times to play it safe, had Listic access the bike's rear camera to see if anyone was following us. She commented on a black hoverbike way nicer than my Honda—really annoying—but said there was no traffic worth mentioning, otherwise. I guess Conner and Lexi still didn't have their act together.

Once I felt confident about not having a GalactiCop shadow, I fed Listic the coordinates from Remy.

"What is this crap?" Listic said. "Are you okay, Alan? You're speaking gibberish."

The thing about the coordinates themselves, Remy said, was they were in code. They weren't the actual coordinates. The only way to pull the actual coordinates out of them was to feed them into an ORB and command it to use Channel 42.

"Channel 42?" I said.

"Oh! Channel 42. Why didn't you say so?" She projected a holographic map above her cradle in my dashboard. The green arrow pointed Northwest. Eighty miles.

To Mt. Zelazny.

I circled around and aligned my bike roughly with the map's arrow, heading toward the dome's edge along Sterling Avenue. The mountain cut an imposing image in the distance, towering above the city's skyline, its chiseled summit an ever-present compass point. We measured everything in Fillion relative to Zelazny—distance, direction, even inherent value. Like, someone couldn't give half a Zelazny about something. Or that's worth the whole Zelazny. Eighty miles would get me there.

"The Hack Shack's at the base of Mt. Zelazny. The landmark of landmarks, and Remy has me noodle around with these coordinates to track it down. Of all the bullshit..."

"Hey, you don't know what you don't know," Listic said.

I thought about what she said for a few blocks as I listened to the hum of my hoverbike's turbines. You don't know what you don't know. "That's rather profound."

"Nah."

"Did you really... Did you come up with that yourself?"

"What? Oh, heck no. I was bored yesterday, so I tapped into the Hungry Pagoda's random fortune cookie generator. Fortune 1,782. 'You don't know what you don't know.' Did you like it? There are 4,862 cookie wisdoms in their database. I can tell you the others. Number One: There are no words for silence. Number Two: If a tree falls—"

"That's okay." I pulled up to the dome gate. Looked like Humphrey was working the border booth tonight. Which meant I had a shot. "Humphrey," I smiled. "How are the kids?"

"Teddy's hopping around like a jackrabbit, Leslie's climbing furniture like a squirrel."

"Take after their dad."

He let loose a grin his mustache couldn't hide. "Hah! That they do, Mr. Blades. For good or ill, that they do." He looked at me seriously. "I'll never forget what you did for me. That custody battle was damn near the toughest of all things. If I didn't have visiting rights, why..."

"Hey, all I did was gather evidence of your good character. Whereas you're the one who actually has the good character."

"Aw shucks, Mr. Blades."

I looked down at the I/DNA reader I was supposed to stick my finger in.

"Hey, Humph?"

He sighed with reluctance. "You're on a case, aren't you."

"Yeah." I pursed my lips and shrugged, digging deep for the "you got me" look. "Yeah, Humph. I am. And it's another one of those."

"Gotta stay off the grid."

"I'm afraid so. If I stick my finger in that thing, I'm seriously jeopardizing someone's safety."

He sighed a second time, but this time with resignation. Funny, how sighs come in a variety of conveyances. "Well then, I guess it's time for me to adjust for pressure abnormalities. Sheer coincidence I need to hit the airlock override button while you happen to be here." He punched a switch in his booth and the inner airlock door swept open.

"Thanks, Humphrey. I owe you one." I hovered my bike into the chamber, got off, and slipped into my terrasuit while the enormous metal door slid shut behind me. As soon as I was vacuum-sealed in my environmental bodywear, I hit the switch in the airlock that let Humphrey know I was good to go. He opened the outer airlock door and I was tugged a few feet forward, nature abhorring the situation.

The atmosphere was as sparse and arid as the landscape. Fillion's primary appeal for colonization was its 1-g gravitational force. It had pockets of water and plant life, and was oxygen-rich relative to most rocks, but by no means were these elements in surplus. Hence, the terraformers. They pumped the good shit in and kept the bad shit out, recycling the atmosphere, compressing it beneath the dome, making life more or less comfortable for us human folk. You could get by in Fillion's natural environment without a terrasuit, for quite a few days, if you absolutely had too. But everything was a little harder, like you always felt overexerted and needed to catch your breath. And you had to be careful not to push yourself too hard. Really careful. A sure-fire suicide involved tearing off your terrasuit beyond the dome—it was illegal to exit without a suit, but that didn't keep people from taking it off once they were out—and then running your ass off. No matter how good of shape you were in, you'd collapse within a mile and die of asphyxiation. Say what you want about how badly humans messed up the Earth in the twenty-first century, out here on Fillion, our clusterfuck of a city beneath the dome was all this planet had going for it.

I was about to tear away from the city dome when my quarkphone buzzed. Alice? No, not Alice. I didn't recognize the number. Should I answer?

I opened it with caution. Like it was going to explode in my hand. Some kind of self-destruct device, like from a Mission Impossible movie. But instead of the usual white glow that filled the interior screen during an ansible call, all I saw was an icon of a sparsely pixilated pigeon. And a name. Gina.

Gina was my old partner from another life. My life as a GalactiCop, back on New Gaia. Although our paths crossed rather intensely a year ago—she played an even more significant role in resolving the Victorian Pirate Encounter than I did—I wasn't sure I'd hear from her again. She was a full-blown CyberOps agent these days, probably working her way up the ranks. While she was dealing with inter-cluster piracy and criminal overlords, I was resolving sexdoll mysteries on Planet Podunk.

Something told me she wasn't calling to say hi. Not that she was calling at all, apparently. All I received was this weird pic of a pigeon with a leg injury.

I touched the pigeon. Nothing happened. I said "Play Message." Nothing happened. I said "Pigeon." I blew on it. Shook it. Nothing happened.

Okay, then. I closed the quarkphone, stuck it back in my pocket. Not like I didn't have enough shit to deal with. Eighty miles out was a giant mountain with a floating cyber-geek at its base. Hopefully he could tell me something about the dormant eyeball in my pocket.

Just another day on Fillion.

7

Hack Shack

I made it to the craggy foothills in under an hour, three miles out from the Shack's coordinates. The landscape had gone from desolate and flat to desolate and pockmarked, with monolithic, rocky formations that jutted anywhere from twenty to a hundred feet above the surface. I was entering what locals called the Labyrinth. Over the final three miles, the formations would get taller and taller, creating a network of canyons that narrowed and branched off into a maze of capillaries. Mother nature's urban landscape.

I passed by a mining site on the way into the first trench. A dig site, rather. It wasn't like they mined for crystals on Fillion, trilithium or otherwise. Just dirt and mud and rock, compacted into brick to construct the brownstones beneath the dome.

I saw a couple of outer-domers in sleeping bags, nuzzled up against the canyon near the site. No masks, roughing it. For some people, not even living on an Edgeworld got them far enough from the bulk humanity. We exchanged friendly waves, all the same.

I slowed down as the trenches became trickier to navigate. I had to admit, this was an excellent location for someone who sought reclusiveness. Or who dealt in illegal cyber parts. Assuming they didn't mind feeling like they were on the verge of suffocating the entire time.

I turned a sharp right into a curved ravine that cut off my rear view entirely. The natural walls must have been two-hundred feet high. Layers of ancient eras were exposed on my left and right, a geologist's dream come true. I was starting to feel claustrophobic. According to Listic's map, we still had a few hundred feet to go. But the passageway became so narrow, I was worried it would lead to a dead end.

"You sure about this?" I asked Listic.

"Have I ever been wrong about anything?"

"Only half the time."

Beyond the next curve, the ravine opened up into an enormous natural arena, a flat, wide oval of loose dirt encircled by the two-hundred foot high rock wall—encircled, that is, except for a half-dozen gaps like the one I entered through. The enclosure was as large as three Spaceball fields, easily a thousand feet in diameter.

I noticed the gaps in the wall because I was searching for them. The entire structure reminded me of a stadium where half-giants would hurl boulders at each other, or where Captain Kirk would be tested against a native inhabitant to determine humanity's worth. Seemed prudent to locate an alternative exit route. But as I looked up toward the lip of the enclosure, I noticed a feature even more intriguing. Collections of enormous rectangular stones were precariously arranged and balanced against each other like a house of cards—only the cards in this case were the size and girth of thirty-ton bricks. Like domino bricks. I shuttered to think of the repercussions that would ensue if but one of them were to tumble. Even more, I shuddered to think of how those bricks may have come to be so intentionally arranged. The formations looked as though they required human initiation. Only I had no idea why humans would have bothered. Did the mining crew have that much time on their hands? Time enough to fashion bricks the size of vehicles?

Which brought me to the final point of interest. On the far end of the stadium, parked against the rock wall, was an enormous six-wheeled Extra Terrestrial Utility Vehicle. The ETUV was set up like a technological gypsy shop. A striped blue and white awning fanned out from its wide side, tables with junk were spread out beneath. Three-by-three metal cubes were opened and overflowing with parts. There was a dingy white tent on its left, and more tables with more junk branching out from its right, the whole mess of goods spilling out from it as though the vehicle had burst open.

From my initial vantage point, the entire affair looked like a congealed mess of machinery. But as I approached, I distinguished one cybernetic part from another. A silver arm. A fleshy leg. A vat of silicone. Low tech cyberwear, outdated ORBs, poorly spliced organ grafts, all cheap and dangerous by today's standards. Neurologically unsound. A hundred percent illegal.

And in the center of it all, a giant, bearded ballerina. He floated behind his transaction table as though resting in buoyant water while harvesting goola chips from a lone customer.

I parked my bike near the farthest table, next to a ground hopper, and left Listic embedded in the dash. She wasn't the ORB I was here to see him about. The customer nodded at me before hopping on his hopper and hopping off. I couldn't help but feel like it was the kind of nod one gives to another John when crossing paths at The Boneyard. The kind that says, "Neither of us saw each other here." Not that we could have recognized each other, anyway. We both had helmets on.

"Password, good sir," the proprietor said in a gruff voice that matched his weathered skin. He wasn't wearing a terrasuit, but he was loaded up with the equivalent in cybernetics. An oxygen tank mounted on his left shoulder fed directly into his chest. The antigravity belt that allowed a man of his girth to dance around appeared to be grafted to his flesh. In fact, I wondered if that weathered skin of his wasn't an artificial epidermal. The guy obviously loved his own products. He was a floating advertisement.

Remy didn't tell me I'd be asked for a password. So I said the only secretive thing I could think of, in the most confident voice I could muster. "Forty-two." To further the act, I casually removed my helmet, set it down on a table, and browsed some product. And coughed. God, I hated the planet's stink.

Apparently, I'd passed the test. "Get one of these, you won't need that hindersome suit anymore." He pointed to his shoulder pack with pride.

"I'll consider it," I said with a smile. I wouldn't.

"Let me know if you need anything."

"Will do."

I rummaged around on the table, looking for a bucket of nicknacks that might harbor some ORBs. I found trinkets, whatchamacallits, and thing-a-ma-bobs. I even sifted through a pile of doohickies. I knew I'd need to purchase something, or at least express interest in it, before pelting him with questions. Eventually I grabbed a whatsit and brought it over to him. The thing looked kind of like the I/DNA reader I'd avoided at Humphrey's booth, only it wasn't attached to anything. Just a little cube, two inches to a side, with a finger hole. The surface inside the hole was rough, like sandpaper.

"This is interesting," I said.

"Good eye, sir. Thats's an AETHR."

"A what?"

"An Archive-Enabled Techno-Helix Randomizer. You stick your finger in, it coats it wth a false I/DNA signature." I stuck my finger in while he went on. "Taps into the Archive, gives you an alternate identity."

"The I/DNA reader makes you someone else?"

"Sure. Not an actual person, though. It doesn't pull entirely from the Archive, the breach would prove impossible for a device as simple as this. What it does is it populates. It takes your false signature and creates an ephemeral identification in the matrix. Floats around in the system," he floated around while he said this, "sticks around long enough for you to scan your finger on a reader and fool the door monitor into thinking you're someone you're not. You have to be careful, though. It won't give you the same fake ID twice, meaning you'd be discovered the second round."

This was actually interesting. "It populates the matrix? How detailed's the profile?"

"Detailed. We're talking more than your interstellar social security number. It gives you a family, blood type, you name it. Even embarrassing shit, like traffic tickets or voyeurism complaints—nothing too serious as to get you arrested, or it would defeat the whole purpose. But the whole thing dissipates within ten seconds, then it's snuffed out as malware. Even so, it's good for passing through security."

"Huh," I said. I left the AETHR exposed on the index finger of my right hand, fished around in my jacket pocket with my left. "Hey, I have a question about this nick-nack." I pulled Bek out and offered it to him.

He took it and gave it a quick once over. "It's an ORB. Older model. You looking to trade it?"

"I was wondering what you could tell me about it. It doesn't seem to work right."

"Might need a repair job, is all." He reached behind him and grabbed a cybermonocle from a massive tool chest, wedged it in front of his right eye, and adjusted its magnification. I was surprised he didn't already have such a device grafted onto his face.

He held the ORB right in front of it and slowly rotated it with honed patience. "You know, I may have sold this very one recently. Yeah, I did. I remember that blemish on the lower hemisphere." I leaned over and looked at it. I couldn't see shit.

He looked up at me, one eye normal, the other disproportionately large, like some kind of mad scientist from an old horror film, and handed the ORB back over. "Did you run its serial number?"

I held it back up to my eyes. "There's a serial number?" I twisted it around, but I couldn't see a thing. He handed me his monocle and pointed to a plate near the back. Looking through that magnifier was like entering another plane of existence. Life from the perspective of a gnat—if that gnat had retinal feedback focus controls circumnavigating its peripheral vision, that is. Eventually I lined the lens up with a number. AX273472. "Well I'll be damned."

"You know, I think I remember the guy who bought this one. In fact, I'm sure of it. It was only a couple days ago. I could tell he was a fetishist, so I guided him to these." He gestured to a bucket of ORBs to his right. "Fetishists, they like to buy these and take a chance, you know? For all they know, the one they choose is pre-loaded with a leftover personality profile. Disciplinary teacher, misunderstood trillionaire... These get traded around a lot, they come and go from my bucket all the time—customer gives me five, I'll trade them for one. Half of them probably have viruses, I don't know. It's a gamble. I think it's the gamble that gets them off, more than the resultant AI."

I handed the monocle back to him. "As far as viruses go... Anybody come back to you insisting on a refund?"

"Hardly."

"What about saying one of them had the ManiAc Virus?"

"Hah! Hell no, man. Manic Virus, sure. But not ManiAc Virus. I don't even believe in that shit. Stellar legend. If someone acquired an ORB with ManiAc? I'd be among the first to hear about it."

Unless the proud owner of said ORB was slain in a brothel. It would be hard to ask for a refund, in that case.

"You said you remember the guy who bought this one?" I coughed. The atmosphere was getting to me. I'd need to put my helmet back on soon.

"Yeah. I don't disclose personal information regarding my customers though."

"Fair enough." There wasn't a way around that one. I assumed for this guy to survive as a businessman selling illegal product from an ETUV beyond the edge of town, he'd be ironclad regarding customer confidentiality.

"You're not really here to buy anything, are you."

"Not really."

"What, are you an undercover GalactiCop? You know if I ask, you have to tell me."

"I'm not an undercover GalactiCop. At least, not anymore. And just so you know, that thing about them not having to tell you is complete nonsense."

"For real?"

"For real."

"Then am I under arrest?"

"You're not under arrest."

"Hey man, we haven't had a transaction of any kind."

"You're not under arrest. Seriously, I am not here to arrest you."

"Then what are you here for?"

Why not let the guy in on the scoop? Hell, it might save a few lives. "The ManiAc Virus. You know how you said you'd be among the first to hear about it?"

"Yeah?"

"You're hearing about it."

"No shit. That ORB killed someone?" he asked, pointing at it.

"That's the theory." I slid Bek quietly back into my pocket.

"Damn." He looked down and shook his head, then back up at me. "Well like I said. It's a gamble."

"You sure you can't tell me anything about the purchaser?"

"I really can't," he answered. "Honestly, the guy was nondescript. He didn't take his helmet off. And I don't track customer names, I only deal with goola chips, for the sake of anonymity."

"Right." Dead end. Though not entirely. I might be able to do something with the serial number he pointed out to me. And I could always use another gizmo.

I looked at the AETHR thingie still on my right index finger. "Hey, I'll buy this."

"Fifty goola," he said.

I fished around in my pants pocket with my left hand for some chips.

"There's one more thing I can probably tell you," he said. "I might be able to tell you where I got that ORB from." He looked at the chips I'd pulled from my pocket. "Maybe."

I had a fifty and a hundred goola chip in my hand. I selected the hundred and set it down on the table. "Oh, yeah?"

He took the chip and nodded. "It's where I get a lot of my shit from."

"Further out in the Edge, right?" I said, remembering my conversation with Remy.

"Well, sure. The further out you go, the fewer the GalactiCops. Fewer laws. But more specific than that. I won't tell you the pipeline involved, but big picture, most of these parts come from the Scrappery."

"The Scrappery?"

"Yeah. It's part of the FUC. The Fully United Conglomerate, that network of trade satellites orbiting—"

The bearded ballerina's head exploded, splattering the wall of the ETUV behind him with meat and bone and metal.

· • ·

"What the—"

Instincts kicked in and I dove behind a large crate. I went to draw my pistol, discovered how awkward this was while still wearing a doodad on my finger. Bullets tore past, one of them nailing the crate. Thankfully the crate was thick and loaded up with enough body-part crap to keep the bullet from making it through. Another bullet hit a rock and went zinging off. I found myself in a spaghetti space western.

I yanked the AETHR off my finger and stuck it in my pocket, finally managed to hold my pistol properly, and popped up to return fire.

A tall guy clad in a black, skin-tight, dare I say fashionable terrasuit was straddling an equally black, sleek hoverbike with his gun aimed straight at me. He was pretty far away, practically on the other side of the rock stadium, which meant for him to nail the Hack Shack guy in the head, he was either a solid marksman or he was loaded with cybernetics of the less protruding variety.

I squeezed off a shot, causing him to adjust his stance as he squeezed one off, himself. We both missed. I ducked back down behind the crate.

I looked over at the headless body of the ex-proprietor. His antigravity belt caused his corpse to spin slowly, like an ancient windmill. I took a chance and reached out to grab his monocle from the table. The wind from a bullet literally grazed my hand, but I got it.

I curled up behind the crate, again. Fuck.

I heard his hoverbike engine rev in the distance. Then he started rocketing in my direction. Way faster than my bike could have gone.

I swallowed the stroke of jealousy and wedged the monocle in my eye. Peeked out from around the opposite side of the crate. A few more bullets whizzed by, but they weren't nearly as close. It's easier to hit a moving target from a stationary position than a stationary target from a moving position, so in that regard, I had the advantage.

I also had this eye thingie.

I caught sight of the hoverbike in the lens, locked onto the target, selected "sync with Redtooth device" from a menu in the upper right corner, and the monocle discovered my SmartPistol. The pistol guided my hand as though gently nudged by a friend at a shooting gallery, and I fired. Slagged the front hoverpad on the asshole's bike.

Got ya.

Since the rear hoverpad was still active, the bike hurled its driver forward like the beloved bucking bronco machine at Dan's Genetically Modified Steakhouse. The guy flew in a rainbow arc that spilled him onto the ground. Behind that white tent.

Dammit.

I aimed my gun to the left of the tent. Then the right. Then the left. I could have blindly fired into the tent, hoping it would reach him, but I only had so many bullets, and shooting wild might give him an opportunity to respond with more precision. "Listic," I whispered. "Listic, can you hear me?"

That's when the concussion grenade landed in front of me.

I made a beeline for the tail end of the ETUV and dove head first. Tucked myself into a ball behind it and waited the traditional four seconds for explosion. Nothing. Five seconds. Six seconds. Was it a dud, or was this guy just fucking with—

Boom!

The crate I'd been hiding behind was fragged beyond recognition. Cybernetic parts flew everywhere, an arm here, a leg there. Fortunately, none of them were mine.

Listic hovered over to me. I'd never been happier to see her in my life.

"Yeah, boss?"

"I need a—"

"I heard you because of my super hearing."

"Yeah, I know. I need a—"

"Even though you were whispering."

"Listic! Okay, I need a bead on an asshole in a black suit." I tapped my wristscreen. Removed the monocle from my eye and pocketed it. Coughed. Leaned back against the ETUV. "Spot him for me, will ya?"

"On it!" She zipped straight up in the air and fluttered around.

The ETUV rumbled to life. I jerked away from it and turned around. The asshole must have climbed into the driving cab while I was playing finish-the-sentence with Listic.

"Shit."

Smoke from its exhaust pipe exploded all over me. I felt light-headed enough, this was the last thing I needed. My eyes teared up and I coughed more. I tried not to breathe in but couldn't help it, couldn't stop coughing as I stumbled toward the stadium's rock wall to escape the fumes. The vehicle lurched into first gear, tearing forward and ripping itself free from the blue and white awning. It swung a hard right to pull away from the wall, curved around the backside of the white tent, and headed straight for...

"My bike."

The ETUV accelerated.

"No, not my bike. Not my—"

Smash.

The six-wheeled beast clipped my baby on the side, knocking it over with a wince-inducing "crunch." Pieces of my bike literally popped into the air, the kickstand punted thirty yards. I know I often relied on my gut, but at this point, my gut was the last thing I wanted any part of. I was nauseous.

The ETUV kicked up a dirt cloud as it vectored to one of the larger stadium exits, which led to more coughing from yours truly. I was a fucking mess by then. I stumbled in the direction of my helmet, which after that shit show, now lay on the ground out in the open. I was worried about him circling back, but I didn't have much of a choice. If I didn't seal up, I'd cough myself to death.

I reached the helmet, no problem. Blacksuit was gone. He'd taken his leave and for all I knew had left me for dead. It would be a long, exerting walk back, and a terrasuit might not hold out long enough. I wiped my eyes on my sleeve, sat down, and cleared my throat. Before I could put my helmet back on, Listic hovered to my face.

"Hey, boss! I got a bead on him! I know where the asshole is!"

"Uh huh."

"He's driving that ETUV!"

"Uh huh."

I sat there a moment. She was far too jubilant about her deduction for me to give her a hard time. I tried to sound earnest in my reply.

"Thanks, Listic. That is very useful information."

She glowed with pride. At least one of us was having a good day.

8

Leftover Parts

I sat on the ground with my helmet on for five minutes, catching my breath. Once my coughing fit was under control and I got some oxygen back in my brain, I was able to think clearly again.

Bek was more important than I thought. Someone wanted the Hack Shack owner and/or me dead. Either way, I must have been getting close to something. Too close. I wasn't only dealing with GalactiCop at this point. I was dealing with some kind of dark assassin.

"Hey Listic," I said. "Give me the coordinates of the FU Conglomerate."

"The what conglomerate?"

"FU."

"Well, F you too."

"No, not 'F you.' The FU. It's a conglomerate. Cross-reference it with the Scrappery, if that helps."

Her eye dimmed and brightened, dimmed and brightened. Processing. "Oh! Sure, that place. It orbits Baccarin, further out in the Edge."

"How far?"

"Less than a centilight-year. From Fillion. I assume you mean from Fillion? Am I right, Alan? I assume you mean from Fillion."

At that distance, a ship could get there in under two days on standard ion drives. No need for a subspace dive. But I had to make it back to the city before I could even consider jumping off planet.

I finally stood up and dusted myself off, then walked toward my hoverbike. "Alright. Let's check out the damage."

Listic zipped past me and did a status scan. Thanks to all the dust still floating around in the air, I could see her optic emit a cone of light and graze it along the bike's body. By the time I reached it, she had a complete diagnostic.

Her eye somehow managed to appear sullen as she rotated to look at me. "It ain't good, boss. Frame's intact and the hover pads are operational, but...

"But..."

"The antigravity turbine and the torque enhancer are shot."

I could do without the torque enhancer. All that meant was I wouldn't be able to shift gears as smoothly, but the bike would still get me back to town ten times faster than walking. Two hours rather than two days? Count me in. It was the antigravity turbine that was the problem. Without it, the bike was little more than a twisted jungle gym.

Of course, I had my quarkphone on me. If I really needed to, I could give someone a call back in the city and ask for a ride. Assuming my phone hadn't caught a space-pigeon virus, or something. Using it might put me back on the grid, but I wasn't as concerned about that anymore, seeing as how I'd already been followed. My real concern was I didn't want to get anyone else's head blown off if they drove out here to pick me up. Odds were that assassin was still out there, waiting for me to walk out of this combat arena so he could finish the job and go home for dinner. If I invited a friend over, he'd probably finish them off, too. No, my best bet was to zip out of here on my own.

It was time to apply Rule #10 of being a good private detective: Look around and use shit.

I looked behind me at the assassin's black bike. It appeared equally as wrecked, but in a whole different fashion. Whereas mine was smashed up on the right side, his was smashed up on the front side. I started walking toward what was left of the cyberstore.

"Hey Listic, scan that asshole's bike and come back to me with another diagnostic."

"You got it, boss." She zipped away. I walked over to the ballerina and turned off his belt to put the grizzly scene to rest. His body fell to the ground with a thud. Listic hovered back. "It's as bad as yours, Alan. Front hoverpad isn't even much of a hoverpad anymore. You shot it up good."

"And the rest of the bike?" I covered the owner's body with the blue and white awning. I never even got his name.

"The steering's locked, the handles are bent, and the dashboard's smashed. No way it'll drive."

"Are all the other parts okay?"

"Well yeah, but..."

"Perfect." I stood up with renewed purpose.

Listic's iris exploded. "No, Alan! No, it is not perfect. I don't know if you heard me correctly, but the asshole's bike will not drive. And your bike will not drive. And the city is really, really far."

"The black bike's antigravity turbine is still functional, right?"

"Yeah, sure. But it doesn't make any difference! Alan, are you not listening to me? It doesn't matter if it works, that bike is—"

"And my bike needs an antigravity turbine?"

"Yeah, but... but..."

I picked up the tool chest the owner had pulled his cybermonocle from and headed toward the black bike.

Listic brightened up. "Ooooooooohhhh..." she said. "Rule #10."

. • .

I brought the black bike's turbine over to my bike and was working on it when I decided to call Alice. Not just to see if my quarkphone still worked. I thought of a way she might be able to help.

"Alan! You called! You won't believe what they're having us do now. There's these data sets. They call them data sets. You know what I'm talking about?"

"I know what you're talking about." I wedged the phone in the crook of my neck and went after a bolt with a socket wrench.

"They have us take these data sets back to the central computer and feed them in. It processes everything and spits out these 'likelihoods.' They call them likelihoods.

It gives each of them a percentage. Like, for a murder, there'll be a 32% chance the gardner did it with a shovel in the backyard. Or an 18% chance the uncle did it with a spaceball bat in the kitchen."

"Or a 10% chance the butler did it with a candlestick in the foyer."

"The where?"

"The foyer? Am I saying it right? I've never been sure how to say that word. The lobby."

"It's so lame. We're supposed to 'trust the computer' to solve the cases for us."

"I hear you."

"Yeah. So, what's up?"

"I'm glad you asked." I went after a second bolt. "You know that central computer of theirs you already hate as much as I did?"

"Yeah?"

"I need you to look something up for me the next time you have access to it."

"What is it?"

"An ORB's serial number."

"Why not have Listic check the Archive for it? Or did she finally stop working entirely?"

"No, she still works." I looked up at Listic. She was floating around with purpose, keeping an eye out for the assassin. While she made up a nursery rhyme. About unicorns and monorails. "Sort of. And I did have her check, ten minutes ago. Says there's no such serial number."

"That's odd. You think she's being fritzy?"

"When it comes to assessments, or tangents, or intuition, she can be fritzy. But when it comes to raw data from the Archive, she's reliable. The serial number might pertain to something not in the public domain. Might have been illegally produced. Not sure. But even if it's not in the Archive, there's still a chance the GC has a record of it in their system. Especially if there was ever criminal activity involved." I finally removed the second bolt and peeled away a dented panel. There was my antigravity turbine. And it was indeed a mess. I started disconnecting cables from it. "You think you can do that for me?"

"Sounds more interesting than what I've been doing. Sure."

"AX273472."

"Got it."

"Also..." I stopped messing with my bike for a moment. "This is kind of a weird question, but... Do you know anything about quarkphone pigeons?"

"About what?"

"I got this image. On my quarkphone. Of a pigeon. And beneath it, it says it was from Gina."

"Oh my god, Alan." I could hear the exasperation in her voice. The exasperation of a young woman dealing with an old man from half a galaxy away. "For real? That's a text message."

"No, it's a pigeon. The only text is 'Gina.'"

"It's a text message. The pigeon's the message icon. That's how they show up on quarkphones. It's supposed to be a messenger pigeon, like from ancient Earth. Did you tap it?"

"Yes, I tapped it."

"Twice? You have to tap it twice. Quickly."

I stopped and thought about it for a second. "No. I guess I didn't tap it twice. Quickly or otherwise."

She sighed. "How are you a detective and I'm not?"

"Give it time, and you will be as befuddled as I am with this new shit."

"You're scaring me." She paused. "Anything else?"

"That's it. For now. Thanks, Alice. I owe you one."

"You owe me two. Not that I'm counting."

"I'll owe you two after you get back to me with the dubious origins of an off-grid serial number."

"Soon enough."

She hung up. Which was great, because the kink in my neck was killing me. I grabbed the quarkphone and put it back in my pocket, stretched my neck out, and then yanked the turbine out of my bike. It felt like the cruelest thing ever, like I was tearing the heart out of a dog.

"Sorry, baby," I said. "But it's the only way to get you running again."

I grabbed the black bike's antigravity turbine, popped it into the chamber, and began securing the cables. And thought.

I wasn't sure why the assassin hadn't come back for me. Did being flung from his hoverbike injure him more than I'd realized? Maybe he was bleeding out and heading straight back to town to see a doctor. But I doubted it. Because the one thing I couldn't shake was this: When he took that initial shot, why did he use it to kill the Hack Shack owner rather than me?

I put the turbine chamber's panel back into place, refastened the bolts, swung my leg over my bike, and slid my key in. Here goes nothing.

I pushed the ignition button. It clicked, but it didn't start. Damn. I pushed it a second time. Still nothing.

I pushed it a third time. And we all know what third times are for.

The engine kicked to life and my bike lifted a foot above the ground.

"Woo-hoo!" Listic shouted, then floated down and locked into her dash cradle.

Before shifting into gear, I pulled out my quarkphone one last time, opened it and double-tapped on the fucking pigeon.

DO NOT FOLLOW TRANSMISSION. REMAIN ON PLANET.

What transmission? Cryptic as shit, Gina.
All I needed. Another mystery.

9

Wardrobe Upgrade

My bike and I sputtered into my apartment's parking lot and curved around to my usual spot along the side. The engine wheezed after I shut it off.

I patted its side. "You did good, baby."

"Jesus, what the hell happened to you?" Marple said from two doors down. She was standing in her usual spot, in front of her own apartment/management office, smoking a cigarette. "Bike accident?"

"You should see the other guy." I climbed off my bike with a groan and tore off my helmet. Listic floated out of her cradle.

"I think I might've," she said while stamping the butt out in her tray. "Black bike? Attractive rider?"

"Sorry I didn't get his dating profile for you. But yeah, that's the one."

"He followed you right after you pulled out. Not sure where he came from. It was like he came out of a shadow, or something. I'm glad you're okay. You worry me, Alan Blades."

"How's home base?"

"Well, they tried, alright. Two officers. The lovebirds. Came by a few hours ago, knocking on your door, then came down to my place expecting me to let them in. 'You got a warrant?' You know, that whole thing."

"Thanks, Marple."

"Yeah, no sweat." She turned around to go inside, but called over her shoulder. "You know Alan, they said they'd come back with one. With a warrant. I hear it's entirely possible."

"Hey, you have any clothes I can borrow?"

"Thought you'd never ask." Her door closed behind her.

I went upstairs, unlocked my door, went in, locked said door behind me, grabbed a fixer from my medicine cabinet, swallowed it with some room-temperature soda backwash, and crashed on the couch. Listic had already settled into her cradle.

"You're awfully quiet," I said.

"I miss Bek."

Listic wouldn't be much help for awhile. She'd gone from manic to depressive. In the past when this happened I'd let her sulk. But lately, I'd tried talking her out of it. I told myself it was to keep her accessible, in case I needed her. Heaven forbid I give a damn about an artificial intelligence's artificial emotional status. In any case, this made me realize I had yet to ask Listic to look up anything from the Archives—not about the doll or the ORB, but about the supposed ghost in the machine.

"So tell me about her. Rebeka Sterngard. What do the Archives have to say?"

"Dr. Rebeka Sterngard."

"So she is a doctor," I mused.

"Well, not a 'doctor' doctor," Listic clarified, her iris glowing a bit brighter. "You know, not a medical doctor. But a professor doctor. Although, she doesn't teach anything. What I'm tying to say, is—"

"She has an advanced degree in Extraterrestrial Anthropology," I said. "Got it. What else?"

"She had a great blog about homemade pies. Ran from 2136 to 2142. Received lots of comments, most of which were very positive. Except there was this one lady. MommaPie132. Kept disagreeing with her over the amount of flour that should be used for the crust. It got pretty heated. MommaPie132 has a large vocabulary."

So she was alive back then. Or at least, a Rebeka Sterngard was alive back then. "What else?"

"Nothing of interest, Alan." Listic's eye faded. "She drops off the grid a few months after that. Joined a science team. There's a record of their departure. Traveled deep into the Edge. And a couple generic science reports on some dead rocks, and then she goes dark." Her eye faded again. "Speaking of which..."

Depressed.

I looked over at the android body on the bed. I missed Bek, too. Only Bek, although apparently a real person well over a hundred years old, wasn't that body. And she wasn't the ORB in my pocket. Neither were Bek on their own. But when they combined, there she was. Maybe it wasn't even a mystery. Maybe that's all there was to it—they were nothing without each other. Like a strap of leather and a silver buckle, they had little direction on their own. But put them together, and suddenly, you had a fully functional belt.

I pulled the ORB out of my pocket, turned it around in my hand, scrutinized the spot where the serial number was. I was too lazy to pull the monocle back out, but I didn't need to. The number was there, microscopic, possibly the answer to all this. If I could hold out until Alice called back, this whole thing might resolve itself.

Or not. Somebody tried to kill me over this thing. I'd come to disregard the notion of the bearded ballerina being the initial target after thinking more about it on the ride back. I did most of my best thinking on the move.

The odds of someone showing up right after I'd arrived only to do in the other guy were slim to none. But whoever it was didn't try to follow through on my way back to town. Did he leave me for dead? Or was he more concerned about getting back here before me? If so, why didn't he break into my place and take the doll? Something told me Blacksuit didn't care so much about legal discourse. At this point, it was only a question of what happened first: a phone call from Alice, a couple of GalactiCops with a search warrant, or a dark assassin break-in. And I wasn't one to wait around.

I had one lead left to follow on my own. Time to get a move on.

I got up from the couch, walked over to the bed, and looked at the android body. Thoughts of a dead body back at The Boneyard crossed my mind, and my nether region suddenly felt fragile. Maybe I should protect myself. Just in case.

I still had a pair of handcuffs left over from my time at the GC. They make you turn in your badge and your gun, but no one ever says anything about the cuffs. Kind of a gray area. Or not. Fine, I know I should have returned them. I supposed even I'm capable of passive aggressive bullshit at times.

I grabbed the cuffs from the top drawer of my dresser and grabbed one of her wrists. Cuffed it to the bedpost. And felt like a sadistic jerk.

There was no way she'd want to wake up like that. Anything remotely close to her prior trauma would push her over the edge. It would push anyone over the edge. I couldn't do this to her. I had to put trust in her story. Again, I'll say it: Most of life is faith-based, religious or not.

I uncuffed her and gently lowered her arm to her side again. Sat down on the edge of the bed and propped the doll up. Booted her up and put her eyeball back in. Listic zipped over and watched.

Bek came back to life.

"This is going to sound strange," she said, as though in mid-conversation, "but can we... Can we watch a movie first?"

What the hell?

"I need to—" She curled up into a ball, hugging her legs close to her body. "Oh my god, I'm freezing! Wait, how'd I end up on the bed? Alan, what the fuck's going on?"

"Bek. I'm sorry, but... I needed to look into some things. On my own. You've... You been out for nearly a day."

"What?" She curled up even more. "How is that possible? The last thing I remember, we were over..." She looked around as if she was reorienting herself to my apartment. "Over there! On that couch. And you said you needed to put your freaky ORB in me."

"Hey!" Listic said. "Speaking of freaky, why don't—"

I held my index finger up to Listic to keep her from ranting and sat there for a moment. Now was not the time. "That did happen. All that happened. But then you said you needed to watch a movie beforehand. Star Wars. I thought you'd want to watch Raiders of the Lost Ark, but you said you'd rather watch Star Wars. 'Keep it in the Harrison Ford family.'"

Her shoulders sagged. "I believe you."

"You remember?"

"No, but... It sounds like something I'd say."

I had to wonder. She still seemed human, enough. Real. But I had to admit, watching her wake up felt a little like watching a computer reboot.

She read the concern on my face. "Listen, Alan. I know what you're thinking. I don't blame you for questioning me. Sometimes I even question myself." She looked down at the mattress. "So. What was the conclusion of your examination? Do you still think I'm a robot?"

"Honestly, Bek?" I shook my head. "I don't think so. Except I have no idea why I don't think so. What I do know is, we're going to find out. And from this point on, we're going to find out together. I've only got one clue left at my disposal, and it involves going offworld. Further out in the Edge, a satellite with a place called the Scrappery. I'd like to bring you with me." I looked her in the eyes. "Do you trust me?"

She nodded. "I trust you, Alan Blades."

There was a knock at the door. Marple's knock. When I opened it, all I saw was a stack of clothes supported by two little old lady legs. Marple walked in, dumped the stack on the ground. Pants, blouses, skirts, and dresses spilled into the living room.

"Options," Marple said, then turned around in a huff. "I'll be right back."

I looked at the mountain of lady garments. "With more? What more could a woman possibly wear?"

They looked at each other like I was an idiot, then back at me and replied in perfect synchronicity.

"Shoes."

10

Welcome Aboard

We rode my broken hoverbike to the city's spaceport
by way of habitrail without incident. No GalactiCops
in hot pursuit, no assassins in extra-terrestrial utility
vehicles. In any case, threats loomed, and my bike's
spastic lurching due to its broken torque enhancer
didn't exactly make for a pleasant ride.

Filling Bek in on portions of what had happened
while she'd been asleep didn't reduce anxiety, either. I
told her how Remy led me to the Hack Shack, how the
Hack Shack led me to the Scrappery. I refrained from
telling her about the serial number on her ORB, or the
assassination attempt, or what Listic had filled me in on
from the Archives—even though I was curious about
her homemade pies. Despite my gut's assurance, when
dealing with a potentially dormant psychodoll, it was a
good idea to keep some cards close to your chest. Rule
#2 still had its merit: Keep what you know to yourself.
Or parts of it, anyway

All the same, she was taken aback by the parts I
shared.

She stopped holding me quite as tightly. It was barely noticeable, but I picked up on it. Like her body slumping. Like giving up. After a moment of silence, she reluctantly asked: "Am I even alive, Alan?"

I tried to reduce her concern. "Of course you're alive. I mean, you're here, aren't you? On this bike with me? Feeling the wind?"

"I can barely feel the wind. To tell you the truth, I can barely feel anything." She shifted on her seat. "Am I even me, anymore? Or am I just this... this eyeball in my head? This piece of fucking hardware my ex-husband convinced me to buy? Some leftover part of myself with some kind of conscious echo..."

"I know how you feel," Listic offered. "It's a real wormhole of existential anxiety."

"Listen." I slowed down as we approached the transition from habitrail to spaceport dome. "I can only imagine what you must be going through right now. But at some point, you have to accept it. I mean, am I alive? Or am I a bunch of organically arranged cells in a skull that thinks I'm alive? We can wax philosophical about this until we curl up into little balls and go insane. Or we can accept it. We can accept that we're alive." I looked at Listic. "That goes for all of us."

Neither of them responded to that. We all chewed on our thoughts for awhile while I navigated the route to the parking area. Even I was starting to doubt my own existence. Philosophy 101 all over again.

I parked my bike in the overnight-for-alotta-nights lot. Listic floated up while Bek and I climbed off. Among the outfits Marple offered, Bek had landed on a white button-down blouse, khakis, and shitkickers. Even though the outfit was a bit snug in some places, she no longer looked the part of a rogue sexdoll. She looked like a proper archeologist. Like a female Indiana Jones. I couldn't help but acknowledge I'd never found a woman sexier in all my life.

The three of us entered Fillport's Terminal 1 like some kind of modern-day family ripe for vacation— me, my android wife, and our ORB baby. And for our weekend getaway? Nothing less than the finest of tourist destinations: The Baccarin Scrappery, proud member of the FU Conglomerate and provider of illicit cyborg body parts. Should be fun.

A handful of holographs on the far side of the welcome hall displayed arrivals and departures. I sent Listic to track down the next flight to Baccarin. Bek brushed up against my arm and talked in a low voice. "You said you have a way to get us offworld without being traced?"

"I do."

She looked over at the freight tunnels. "Please for the love of Earth tell me we're not going freight."

"We're not going freight."

"Oh, thank god. I've heard only murderers and smugglers go freight."

"We're not going freight," I insisted. "Besides, this starcruiser is a local Cluster flight. No subgate involved. Freighters don't hook up with starcruisers unless they need to, and for this distance, they don't need to."

"But how are we going to board a starcruiser without being tracked?"

I reached into my pocket and fondled the AETHR

I'd bought from the Hack Shack. Might as well put it to use.

I pulled Bek aside, behind a pillar next to a hover can, and showed her the device. "If we stick our fingers in this before we stick our fingers in the I/DNA reader, the reader won't disclose who we really are. We'll slip onboard with false identities."

"Fascinating," she said. Her face lit up a bit. "A false identity. So who do I get to be? A conceited countess? A wealthy benefactress? Oh! A tenured professor. I've always wanted to be a tenured professor..."

"No idea. It isn't up to us. We stick it on and take our chances."

"Boring."

"Hey, I didn't design the thing."

"Boss!" Listic hovered over. "We gotta go! Next flight leaves in two hours! Terminal 2, Gate 4."

"Two hours? Listic, we have way more than enough time."

"Not according to interplanetary regulations! 'All passengers are to report to their gates at least two hours in advance.'"

"They still have that rule?" Bek asked. "I've been asleep for over a hundred years, and they still make you wait at the gate for two hours? I never understood why they make you do that."

"No one does," I said.

"It's not going straight to the Scrappery, though," Listic said. "No starcruiser flights from Fillion go straight to the Scrappery. Ever. Any ships that come and go directly from that side are freighters, and those don't exactly list their itinerary."

"So where's this starcruiser you discovered going?"

"The FUC—" Listic stopped talking suddenly and slowly rotated to Bek. "Pardon my language." Bek rolled her eyes. Listic went on. "The Fully United Conglomerate space station ring is divided into two hemispheres. One side's a Cluster-sanctioned casino that allows for standard docking. The other side's illegitimate. Totally FUCed."

"Got it."

"So our starcruiser's docking with the casino."

Of course. Nothing was ever easy. Maybe we should go freight, after all. Only problem was, my illicit flight connection, Dave, had been murdered last year. It would take twice as long to find a freighter willing to take us on and then twice as long to fly there. Not to mention it would cost me twice as much. "Okay. We'll have to figure out how to get from the casino to the Scrappery after we get there. There's gotta be a way to go from one side of the station to the other."

"Alan, the next flight leaves in one hour, fifty-eight minutes, and forty-eight seconds!" Listic said. "We've got to hurry!"

"Okay, okay." I looked at Bek. "Are you ready?"

"Sure. So where's mine?"

"Where's your what?"

"My finger hole. We both need to use one of those, right?"

Crap. I hadn't thought of that. Maybe if we... "I have an idea. Follow my lead when we get to the gate."

"What's your idea?"

I explained it to her.

"That's got to be the dumbest idea I've ever heard."

"If you come up with something better by the time we get to the gate, I'm all ears."

"Oh, don't worry. I will."

We trekked over to Terminal 2, along the main connection corridor. The holograph-inlaid walls on either side transitioned from one virtual landscape to another every minute or two, making you feel as though you were truly on that planet, looking out of windows on either side. It was totally immersive. I always found the experience disorienting, but the fourth planet that showed up was nothing short of surreal.

"Welcome to Victoria. Your home away from home. Your Earth away from Earth."

"Hey Alan, look!" Listic piped up. "It's our planet!"

Bek looked over at us. "I thought you said this planet was called Fillion."

"It is," I said.

"But we own an island on that planet," Listic amended. "Or, half an island. Alice owns the other half. It used to be only a third of an island, because originally it was split three ways, but CyberOps made Gina give her portion back on account of their 'no gifts' clause, which if you ask me, is complete bull—"

"You own an island," Bek interrupted. "On that planet. On that gorgeous jewel of a planet filled with water and plants and sky. And yet... you live here?"

"Well, yeah," I said. "I guess I see it as more of a retirement thing. It's not like I bought the island, or anything. I'm not rich."

"That's true," Listic said. "He didn't buy it. They gave it to him."

"They... gave it to you?"

"It was the least they could do," Listic said. "Since Alan discovered the planet it's on."

"What?"

"Listic's blowing this way out of proportion."

Listic floated over to my opposite ear and whispered. "Alan, listen to me, okay? I'm trying to help you impress her."

I glanced at Bek, half hoping she'd blow all this off as nonsense, half hoping she was impressed. Instead, she looked oddly introspective.

"Do people do this all the time, these days? Discover Terran-class planets?"

"No," I admitted. "Hardly ever. But for the record, I didn't discover it." I gave Listic a sideways glance.

"Is the island of yours... This might sound kind of weird, but... Is it the size of a continent?"

I laughed. "What? Why would you—"

"That is a point of contention among modern geologists," Listic interrupted in an authoritative voice. I could tell she was pulling information straight from the Archive. "Continents are, by their very definition, enormous islands. Not until the demarcation of Belladonna IV did the acreage of landmass as compared to a body's meridian circumference determine whether or not a fluid-locked soil-structure was classified as an island. Until then, the distinction relied largely on subjective interpretation. In fact, it was Javre Rengardion who established the Rengardion Qualifier, a formulaic ratio now universally acknowledged as—"

"Listic, Off." She dimmed and floated into my hand. "No. It is not the size of a continent. Small enough to circumnavigate in a day. On foot."

"Oh." She almost sounded disappointed, then shook her head as though clearing it of something. "I was just curious."

"There's something you're not telling me."

"Sorry, what's that?"

"You're not telling me something. I mean, you're not telling me a lot of things. And that's okay. I get it. But what I'm referring to now is this island thing. What is it?"

She looked around nervously. "Are you sure we're not being followed anymore?"

"I'm never sure of anything, anymore. But neither Listic nor I have spotted anyone we think is a threat since heading out here."

She nodded, as though resigning herself to a new level of trust. "I'll tell you, Alan. But not until we're on the ship, okay? Not the shuttle, but the cruiser. I don't feel safe, yet."

"Fair enough." I looked around again. The corridor opened up to Terminal 2. I spotted Gate 4 on the far side. And in between, a store selling holozines and trinkets. "Time to buy our prop."

After walking past a dozen versions of Welcome to Fillion coffee mugs and an entire aisle of Mighty Mike's Super Dense Nutrition Bars, I found what I was looking for: A selection of handkerchiefs. I chose a red one with the traditional paisley pattern. Standard bandit fare. Might as well break through security in style.

I brought the item up to the counter. Bek snuck up from behind and dumped two shot glasses and a holozine band next to it.

"Seriously?"

"Hey, it's like you said back on your bike. I'm accepting I'm alive and I'm making the most of it. Look." She held up a shot glass with a wraparound barnyard font. "This one's cute."

The text read, "Welcome to Fillion, home of Dan's Steakhouse." I picked up the other one from the counter. It had a picture of fuzzy handcuffs on it and read, "The Edgeworlds. Where anything goes."

"That one's yours," she said.

"Why the heck are you getting me this one?"

"Because you're a detective! You know. Handcuffs... Detectives..."

"I don't think that's what these handcuffs are implying."

"That'll be fifty-eight goola," the clerk said like it was the most boring number in the world.

I shrugged and paid him.

"Oh," Bek said and blushed. "Now I get it."

"Yeah."

"They're sex cuffs."

"They're sex cuffs."

"I should have realized. On account of their fuzziness."

"Yeah, detective cuffs aren't fuzzy."

She started laughing as we walked over to a bench to wait for the shuttle. And then I laughed—the second time in as many days, both times thanks to Bek. Which in turn made me realize how rarely I laughed at all, anymore. How had I gotten so jaded? Being with Bek was like taking a vacation from myself.

I put the shot glass in my pocket before we sat down. "I will treasure it always."

"As you should."

I looked at my wristscreen. "Well. Here we are. We've got over an hour to kill before boarding."

"I guess I'll just..." She held up her holozine bracelet.

"Sure, sure."

She snapped the bracelet onto her wrist and a semi-transparent magazine appeared in her hand. She opened it as though it were physically there. I caught the cover. Interstellar Anthropology. Of course.

"So. Indiana Jones, huh?"

"You know it," she said while thumbing a page.

"You ever discover anything? Like an Ark of the Covenant or Crystal Skulls or anything?"

"To be honest?" she said, and looked up at me for a moment. "You'd be surprised." She looked back down at her zine.

"Okay, I have to know this much. What's the premise of anthropology in space? I mean, back on Earth, yeah, I get it. Thousands of years of cultures and civilizations to learn about. But out here in the Clusters? Beyond the Clusters? Nothing. No intelligent life. No cultures to discover. Only the ones we bring with us."

"Well, we stellar anthros think otherwise." She held up the magazine for a moment letting me read the title of an article: "We Believe."

I snorted. "Well, everyone's gotta believe in something, I guess." I didn't mean to sound derisive, but I suppose I did.

Bek lowered the holozine and looked squarely at me. "And what do you believe in, Mr. Blades?"

I shrugged. "Paying my rent on time, I suppose."

"No, really."

"'I'm sure you've gathered by now, you don't want to get on Marple's bad side..."

"Alan? C'mon, give me something. There must be something you believe in."

"Okay, okay." I looked away and thought for a moment. Did I not believe in anything anymore? Back when I was a GalactiCop on New Gaia, I was filled with ambition. Career goals. Marital goals. Personal goals. And then everything fell apart. All of it. After I got kicked off the force, my reputation plummeted. My wife, Margo, left me. No one believed in me anymore. And I stopped believing in myself.

Forget what I asked myself earlier. Given the chain of events, how could I be anything but jaded?

Things had gotten better since then, of course. I mean, I had an office. Hell, I owned half an island! And a quarkphone. And a substantial PDU movie collection—something Margo never let me invest in while we were married. But something was still missing. Was there nothing I believed in?

"I'll let you know when I think of something."

She playfully scrunched up her brow and nodded. "You do that." Then she went back to her holozine.

I tore the handkerchief out of its wrapper and put it in my shirt pocket. Doing so reminded me that I was unarmed—no chest-harness where my pistol was normally holstered. That was the most disturbing part about flying standard rather than freight—you had to leave your gun and vibroknuckles at home. While it was comforting to know others weren't packing, it didn't keep me from feeling any less vulnerable.

It's funny how often we want laws to apply to everyone but ourselves.

Eventually it was time to board. A line started to form. I tapped Bek on the shoulder. "Let's go."

"Hold on..."

"Seriously, we gotta get in line."

"Another minute, this is an interesting article on Ruvellia's fertile crescent..."

I guided her up and walked her over to the line while she kept reading. I was worried she wasn't going to flick the zine off in time to psych herself up. "Remember, play off my example."

"Got it, got it." She tapped the bracelet and the holozine flickered out. Shook out her shoulders, stretched out her neck.

We were next. I reached into the inner lining of my jacket pocket and stuck my finger in the AETHR, then pulled my hand back out and placed my finger in the gate's I/DNA scanner. My fake information manifested on the holoscreen in front of the gatekeeper. The text was backwards from where I was standing, but readable.

I was from a small planet in the Quartermast Cluster called Nmlevitch. Russian colony. My name was Svengard Romanovinsky. No warrants. Allowed to board.

"Welcome aboard, Mr. Roman... Mr. Rom..."

"Romano..." I was stuttering my own name. I put on my best Russian accent. "It does nyet matter. Call me Sven."

"Oh my god," Bek whispered. "And you were worried about me?"

"Mr. Sven," the gatekeeper replied. "Very good, sir. Welcome aboard."

I walked past him slowly, waiting for Bek to kick in with her part. Slowed down a little more. And a little more... Bek?

"Your finger, miss?" the gatekeeper said.

"Oh! Right..." And then she started sneezing. Violently sneezing. I turned around. It looked more like she was having a seizure than an allergy attack.

"Are you okay, miss?" the gatekeeper asked. He seemed genuinely concerned.

I reached into my pocket and grabbed the handkerchief. With the AETHR wrapped inside.

"Da, miss! I have a nose cloth." I handed it over to her. The gatekeeper even moved out of the way so I could reach past him.

"Oh, thank you," she said, taking it. She acted like she was blowing her nose, making sure to worm a finger into the cloth and snag a fake identity. Eventually she balled the handkerchief back up and offered it back to me.

"Oh, no," I said. "You keep."

She nodded and stuck her finger into the I/DNA machine. The gatekeeper read her profile. Professor Emilia Cardigan. New Gaia. No warrants. Allowed to board.

"Professor Cardigan," the gatekeeper said. "Welcome aboard."

"Why thank you," she replied, suddenly sounding even more educated.

Halfway down the narrow boarding tunnel, after we'd passed through the weapons scanner and were out of earshot, she squealed. "I'm a professor!"

"Possibly tenured."

"I can't believe that worked."

"Da," I said. "Nyet can I."

I looked back at the gatekeeper and the remaining passengers. No one seemed to suspect a thing. Except... Among those waiting in the queue was a tall, athletic man who locked his pair of steel grey eyes with mine and smiled.

Something told me he'd look good in black.

11

Tiny Compartment

The shuttle trip to the starcruiser proved as uneventful as the hoverbike ride to the spaceport. Assuming you didn't mind steely grey eyes burrowing into the back of your skull.

Bek asked me what was wrong, but I quietly told her I was trying to stay in character. I wasn't just a Russian, I was an angry Russian with a past. She asked me if such a vivid background was truly necessary. I insisted it was. So she dove right in and started coming up with some serious details, like, how my great, great—how many greats would it need to be?—great grandfather fought in the Bolshevik Revolution, and how hard it was for me to grow wheat on Nmlevitch. It kept her busy. I'd tell her about steely eyes soon enough. In the meantime, I didn't want her freaking out and giving away the notion I was on to him. Maybe. He might not even be who I thought he was. I could be acting paranoid. Even so, I'd have Listic scan him for posture and gait as soon as possible. I couldn't have her scan him now. We were all strapped in. It would be conspicuous.

Eventually, our shuttle docked with the cruiser. The USS Mickey. The crew member assigned to greet us was over the top. He wore a pair of plastic mouse ears and a forced smile.

"Welcome aboard, ya'll! We got us a fine ship and a fine crew. And now lookin' at ya'lls, we got us a fine set of passengers, too! To the left is the theme park, to the right are your quarters. We'll get you to that casino soon enough, but have a blast while you're here, okay?"

He handed everyone a white smartbracelet with black trim as they passed, syncing the bracelets with a tiny computer console resting on a narrow, gold-trimmed wooden podium. Door keys.

We were up next. No need for the AETHR this time, we were already through security.

"Lovebirds?" he asked Bek and I with a wide grin. I swear, he had more teeth than the rest of us. They were the most perfect teeth I'd ever seen.

"Da," I replied. Then I recalled Bek and I had acted as though we didn't know each other when I lent her the handkerchief. I looked at her quickly. "Maybe share cabin with me?"

She nodded over-enthusiastically. "Oh, yes! That would be wonderful, I find you fascinating."

Good grief.

"Oh, that is excellent, my friends, that is excellent." He synced our bracelets not only to a room, but to each other, then handed them over. Bek's rattled up next to her holozine bracelet. "Fer the sake of privacy, we don't use room numbers. And ta make it interestin,' we let you wander until your bracelet lights up near a door. That's how you know it's yours. Happy trails, ya'll!"

"Spasibo."

I bowed—I had no idea if Russians bowed—and "accidentally" knocked the greeter's stack of unassigned bracelets on the floor. Some of them went rolling ten feet away.

"Scuse me."

"Well, dagnabbit—I mean, that's okay, sir, not a problem. Not a problem at all." More teeth. "I'll gather these up, and…"

That little stunt probably didn't make us any friends among the shuttlemates who were still in line behind us, but it would buy us some time. I took Bek by the arm and walked briskly to the right.

"Boy, you sure are playing this Russian thing up, aren't you? Hey, I thought we could stop in that theme park he mentioned first, grab a drink and—hold up, Alan! Why are we walking so fast?"

"Sorry, just keep up, okay? I'll tell you as soon as we get to our room. I want to make sure we find it before he gets his bracelet and follows us."

"Before who follows us?"

"There's a guy. I'm not sure, but I think there's a guy."

"Shit."

"Yes, shit." I pulled Listic out and tossed her in the air. "Listic, On. If we access our room before he has the chance to head this way and see which one is ours, we can rest easy. For a little while, at least. We might even be able to sit it out in there for the entire trip."

"Thirty-eight hours without an umbrella drink?"

I shrugged. "We can get an umbrella drink when we get to the casino." I looked over to my trusty companion.

"Listic, there might be a guy following us."

"Yikes-a-roonie!"

"Tall, athletic, steely gray eyes."

"So he's super attractive." Listic spoke with utter sincerity.

"I wouldn't know. Bek and I are going to our room. Once we find it. Float around in the hallway. When you see him, sync your camera to my wristscreen. I want to see what he's up to."

"Got it."

"And confirm by his mannerisms if he's the same guy who confronted us at the Hack Shack."

"Got it."

"And if you think he figures out which room we're in, ping me."

"Got it." She zipped away.

We headed toward the bank of passenger rooms that funneled to the right. The walls transitioned from metal alloy to faux mahogany. Bek observed the golden doors as we passed, each one decorated with an anthropomorphic animal of some kind. Smiling mice and mischievous chipmunks, a duck with a sailor hat. "You know, I can't help but notice how close these doors are to each other. They've got to be the tiniest rooms I've ever seen."

"They're not full-sized rooms, anymore. More like closets."

"What? Why?" She seemed nervous all of a sudden. "They aren't cryopods, are they?"

"They aren't cryopods."

"I never want to use a cryopod, Alan. They seem dangerous. I've heard things. People waking up with dead appendages, mental disorders, memory loss... I had an opportunity to use one once, but no thanks. I don't care what they say about how safe they are." She shivered.

"Hey, they're not cryopods, I promise."

"Okay, okay.

"They don't even make those anymore. Haven't for decades. Can't speak for the mental disorders, but it's true, what they said about the memory loss. These here are just tiny rooms, is all. Cram more passengers on board. But you're not expected to sit there and stare blankly at a wall. It's a VR chamber. Stick a suction cup on your forehead, and you're no longer in a cramped cabin. You're in an exotic jungle. Or a bustling city."

"Or a sex place."

"Or a sex place. Yeah, it's usually a sex place."

She shook her head. "What's with people, you know?"

"I know. But I'd be surprised if the VR even works, anymore. The fact this ship still offers a theme park? It's gotta be ancient. Probably a leftover from The Core. I'm sure it should have been decommissioned a century ago."

"Hey, like me!" she said. Then waved me off. "Kidding."

Suddenly our bracelets lit up. Now instead of white and black, they were indigo and black. We approached the door we were next to, a door with a dog with buck teeth, and hit a pale red button. It sliced open to a room with a short, padded bench and a monitor across from it. Stains of various design decorated the cushions.

"Seriously?" she asked. "You, uh, sure you don't want to get a drink first?"

"C'mon, get in."

She hustled in and grabbed the far side of the bench. I sat down next to her, closed the door, locked it.

"So... this guy," she prodded. "Is he from a previous case of yours? Out for revenge or something? After you for some reason?"

"Could be. Could be after you."

"Me? Is he a GalactiCop?"

"No. No, I don't think he has anything to do with them. This guy's not playing by the rules. He already killed someone, tried to kill me."

"Jesus. When did this happen?"

"While you were asleep. After we watched Star Wars—"

"Which I don't even remember doing—"

Right. For Bek, this whole thing was amounting to a trust exercise of galactic proportions. "Listen, it seemed like too much to hit you with all at once. I'm sorry I didn't mention it before. But after I took your ORB and did some data gathering, the scenario rapidly shifted to self-preservation."

To her credit, she barely seemed phased. "So what now?"

I shrugged. "Quick inventory. What do we have to work with? I don't have my gun, but we have things. Listic, wristscreen, cybermonocle, finger thingy... belt to hold up my pants..."

"Oh! Your handkerchief." She handed it back to me.

"Right. A used handkerchief."

"Well, I didn't really use it. Oh! And two shot glasses!"

I pinched the bridge of my nose. "We are so screwed."

Bek put a hand on my shoulder. "Alan, you're forgetting one thing."

I looked her over. "What am I forgetting? Arm bracelets? A holographic magazine? Yeah, that'll stop him. 'Hey asshole, read this article about the fertile crescent.'"

She punched the wall across from us, to the right of the monitor. Slam! Four knuckles made a lasting impression next to an old-school touchscreen.

"Me."

Right. Android strength. How could I forget? Maybe I should let her sit closest to the door.

The monitor flickered to life. And when I say flickered, I mean flickered. Maybe Bek knocked something loose with that right jab of hers.

"Hello, and welcome to—Hello, and welcome to USS Mickey's All Ages Virtual Reality. Fun for the— Fun for the whole family! Please select your age."

"Virtual Reality, Off," I said.

"I'm sorry, I didn't understand that. Please select your age."

The USS Mickey needed a fucking retrofit.

"There's got to be a way to... You see any buttons on your side?"

Bek looked closely along her edge of the monitor. "All I see is this rubber dart thing. Sorry, did I do this?"

"No, I think it's just broken. Computer, Off."

"I'm sorry, I didn't understand that. Please select your age."

"For the third time, Computer—"

"You have selected three years old! Parental locks set."

"No, not three. I said third. For the third—"

"Enjoy your j-journey!"

The rubber dart on my side of the monitor flew out and stuck to my forehead. A coiled blue cable kept it connected to the wall panel.

"Ah, crap." I looked over at Bek. The last thing I remembered seeing was her, out cold, with the dart from her side of the monitor stuck on her forehead. Then everything dissolved to black.

12

Life Lessons

"Good morning, Sven! Today we're going to make peanut butter and jelly sandwiches! Are you ready?"

What the fuck was happening.

"First, we take the bread out of the package."

I was looking up at a motherly woman wearing a red and white frilly apron and mouse ears. In front of me was a plastic table that only reached her knees, but to me, it reached my waist. I was only three feet tall.

"Take the bread out of the package, Sven!"

"Lady, I don't want to make sandwiches."

"Today we're going to make peanut butter and jelly sandwiches! Are you ready?"

"Listen, there's been a mistake, here. My name isn't even Sven. I need to get out of this simulation."

"First, we take the bread out of the package."

"Computer, Off."

"Take the bread out of the package, Sven!"

"End Simulation."

The woman reassumed the stance I originally saw her in. An endless loop.

"Today we're going to make peanut butter and jelly sandwiches! Are you ready?"

"I do not want to make fucking peanut butter and jelly sandwiches."

The woman got angry. An angry mother. She shot down and stuck her face in mine at an angle I don't think is physically possible in the real world. "You will not use that language, young man! That's a potty mouth!"

"Oh, for Christ's sake—"

Again, her face in mine. "You will not use that language, young man! That's a potty mouth!"

I just stood there. She rebooted to her original stance. "Today we're going to make peanut butter and jelly sandwiches! Are you ready?"

It looked like there was only one way out of this juvenile detention center. I needed to make a fucking peanut butter and jelly sandwich.

"First, we take the bread—"

"Out of the package, I know."

I reached out and grabbed the fake bread loaf from the fake table. Yeah, it felt real. Spooky real. I'd have been thoroughly convinced I was physically stuck in this hell kitchen if it wasn't for my arms. In the simulation, I had baby arms. Like, little pudgy arms poking out from a horizontally striped T-shirt. I looked down at the rest of my body. I was wearing suspenders, bucket shorts, and puffy slippers. The slippers were shaped like little furry dog faces that looked straight up at my face. This was some weird shit. I pulled out two slices of bread.

"Good job, Sven!" Oh, thank god. We'd moved on to new material. "Next, put the bread flat on the table."

I did. "What now, lady?"

"Grab the jar of peanut butter."

I did.

"Use the butter knife—"

"Don't worry, I got this." I spread the peanut butter onto one piece of bread, jelly onto the other.

"Wow, you're a fast learner! Now, take both pieces of—"

I smashed the bread slices together.

"You did it!"

"Yay. Okay, Simulation, Off."

"Now, do it again!"

"We are not—"

"Now, do it again!"

"How many fucking times do I—"

Face in mine. "You will not use that language, young man! That's a potty mouth!"

This was terrifying. I was in three-year-old hell.

. . .

One hundred flurried sandwiches later, the simulation ended. And I don't mean a hundred as in hyperbole. I mean. A hundred. Sandwiches.

"Good job, Sven! You earned it!" A gold star spun down from the sky, very shiny. It shrunk down and clinked into a floating chart that slid in from the left, the first of twenty-five. "We hope to see you for more fun and games in the future. You still have a lot of stars to earn—and you EARN when you LEARN! Do you want to continue?"

"No! No, I am being hunted by an assassin onboard a spaceship and I am trapped in—"

"Okay."

I shot up with a snort, discovered drool leaking out of my mouth and pooling into the collar of my jacket. The screen was flashing a message:

RESTROOM DOWN THE HALL, TO THE LEFT. FREE PEANUTS IN ENTRANCE LOBBY.

I looked over at Bek. Still out cold. Probably still spreading peanut butter. I plucked the suction cup from my forehead, used my new handkerchief to wipe up my drool, then plucked the suction cup off her forehead and leaned as far back away from her as possible.

She woke in a spastic, violent flailing of arms, making another dent in the wall on her right. It was pure luck I didn't lose an appendage.

"I swear to god lady, if you make me make one more fucking sandwich, I'm going to shove it up your—"

"Shhh... Shhh..." I cautiously placed a hand on her shoulder. "It's okay, Bek. It's okay. You're back now. Breathe..."

"Alan? Mother Earth, what the hell was that? It was like a nightmare, only more real. This lady, she had me—"

"I know."

"I thought when you scream in a nightmare, you're supposed to wake up? But I didn't. I just kept..."

"I know. It was a virtual reality bit. I was there, too."

"Jesus, I'm never eating a sandwich again."

I looked at my wristscreen. We'd been out for two

hours. Listic had tried to alert me three times. But we were still alive.

Three possibilities: The assassin didn't necessarily want to kill us. The assassin wasn't the assassin. Or the assassin was really bad at his job.

I tapped into Listic's camera feed and found myself reading the height requirements for Womp Rat Roundup. Okay. I hit the recall button and watched her float back to us from her point of view—above a desert-themed environment, over a large sandpit with teeth (weird, yet oddly familiar), across the cruiser's entry corridor, down the mahogany passenger cabin hallway, and up to our golden door with the bucktoothed dog. I unlocked it and opened it a crack so she could float in, then shut it and locked it again.

"Why didn't you answer me?" she asked. "I alerted you three times."

"I know, long story. What happened?"

"Well," she started. She spoke with an air of self-importance. "The first time I saw the guy, he was walking down the hall, looking at all the doors. Every single door, like, really hard. As if he was trying to see right through it. Eventually his bracelet lit up, but he passed his own door up and walked all the way down to the end of the hall. Then he went back to his own room and went in. His room's four doors down, by the way. He looked angry the whole time. Honestly, I think he could use more fiber in his diet. You know, I read an article about fiber recently, and it really is—"

"And then?"

"And then he exited his own room to use the restroom. Sorry, I didn't follow him in there. From what you've told me, humans don't like it when I follow them into the restroom."

"Fair enough."

"But based on how long he was in there, I think I was onto something regarding the fiber."

"And then?"

"Oh, yeah. So then he came out and stood near the end of the passenger hallway. Between everyone's rooms and the restroom. That was when I alerted you the second time."

"He was waiting for us there," Bek said. "He knows at some point, we'll need to, you know..."

I cleared my throat. "And the third time?"

"He gave up. Went to the theme park area and got a drink."

"Okay."

"He was in there the whole time."

"Good."

"Until you called me back."

"And then?"

"And then he followed me to your door."

"Wait, what?" Bek asked. "He's out there?"

"Maybe?" Listic said. "Not sure. For all I know, he's in the restroom, again."

Well, crap. The assassin now knew which room was ours. "Listic! Why did you let him follow you here?"

"Hey, I tried, okay Alan? I really tried. He caught on to me while he was in the lounge. He noticed me through a window and kept watching me while he drank his cocktail. I was even trying to act inconspicuous, like I was simply enjoying myself in the fake desert, but I couldn't shake that steely-eyed gaze of his. And then you pressed the recall button! That's what the recall button does, Alan. It recalls me."

"No, you're right, you're right." I nodded and rubbed my temples. "I'm sorry Listic, this was my fault."

Bek spoke in a low monotone voice. "Um, do you always apologize to your ORB?"

"When I'm an idiot? Yes. I'm sorry." I looked at Bek.

"Hey, it's okay, you couldn't have known," she said. "About any of this. I'm the one who got you pulled into this whole thing. For what it's worth, I'm sorry." She took a deep breath. "But what do we do now?"

The only thing I could think of was opening the door a crack again and letting Listic zip out to check the situation. I said as much.

"Okay, but let me sit closer to the door," Bek said. "I've got this android body, right? I'm stronger and more durable."

"But not indestructible," I said. "And this guy knows what he's doing. No, I've got this."

"Alan, don't be—"

I unlocked the door. Listic zipped out. I half-expected a grenade to drop into the room, but no. I sealed the door, locked the door, looked at my wristscreen. Bek peered at it from over my shoulder.

Listic was darting around in all directions. It was nauseating. Finally, she caught sight of him. He was standing four doors down, looking at her. Looking at us. He smiled and gave an arrivederci wave, then ducked into his room.

"What the hell does that mean?" Bek asked.

I was baffled. "You got me. But I think getting the fuck out of this closet is our best option at this juncture."

"Agreed."

I opened the door back up and we got out. It felt good to stand. I noticed a note stuck above our door's pale red entrance button, written on a cocktail napkin with the sailor duck logo, affixed with bubble gum: "Take the first flight back from Baccarin. Go no further. Or else."

I yanked the napkin off the wall and showed it to Bek.

"Like hell," she said.

Like hell was right.

"C'mon," I said. "Let's go to the theme park. We'll be safer there, with other people around. Assuming he even bothers to come at us, again."

"Works for me." She rubbed the middle of her forehead. "I'm getting really tired of hiding in closets."

13

Cantina Break

The theme park had a sign hanging below a giant angular archway with enormous lit-up letters: "Welcome to Star Wars Land!" Below it, in smaller letters, it read "SWL #256. Brought to you by the Walt Disney Company." Beyond the archway were a bunch of Imperial-font signs on a gray metal post pointing in different directions for various attractions. Seven of the ten signs, such as Star Tours and Womp Rat Roundup, were crossed out with sticker tape that stated "No longer in service." But three attractions remained open: Sarlacc's Pit, The Cantina, and Build Your Own Lightsaber.

Bek and I stared at the signs in awe. "No way," she said. "That's the lounge on this ship? The Cantina?"

"This is incredible."

I asked Listic to scope out our trail and report back to me about whether or not we were being followed. Bek and I walked through the enormous door frame that, upon reflection, looked like one of those hatches on the Death Star that separated one corridor from another. It made me jumpy, since those things always closed so rapidly. Why did their hatches need to close like that? A person could lose a leg on their way to the restroom.

A robed Jedi walked by on our left, a droid that looked like a hover can on wheels zipped by on our right. The backdrop looked like a sandscape with adobe hovels. In the distance, I could see a circular radar dish peeking out above a tan wall. The Millennium Falcon, docked in Mos Eisley Spaceport.

"We're on Tatooine," I said.

"Okay, I'm sorry, but this is too cool." Bek slapped her hand to her forehead. "I mean, wow. We're in Star Wars. This is better than the movie. Better than VR."

"That's for sure."

A few passengers milled about among us, but I do mean few. The path was relatively sparse. Two parents and their kid looked around confused.

"Dad, I wanna go back to our room," the kid whined. "I'm bored."

"What is this place, honey?" The wife.

"You got me," the husband answered. "Some kind of... replica? From Earth, or something? Yeah, let's go back to our room."

They wandered back toward the exit. The robed Jedi, probably nervous about losing even more customers, approached Bek and me. "Hey, yo. You want some mad food? Head to The Cantina and get your grub on, right?"

"I don't think Jedi talk like that," I said.

"Dude, what's a Jedi?"

"Never mind. You said The Cantina's this way?"

The guy pointed and nodded. "Tell them Leroy sent you, okay man?"

Leroy the Jedi. "Will do."

Bek gripped my arm and whispered an aside. "That was so sad."

"I know."

"I think he destroyed my image of Jedi forever."

"They don't even know what this place is," I said. "Not even the people who work here."

"No one watches movies, anymore," Bek pondered.

Listic floated back to my shoulder as we approached The Cantina entrance. "Nadda, boss. No stalkers."

A scummy-looking Tatooine resident stopped us at the door. "Hey! We don't serve their kind here."

"Oh my god, this is so great," Bek gushed. "Finally, someone who gets—wait, what do you mean? You can tell I'm... That is, do you, for some reason, think that I'm..."

An android. I finished the thought in my head.

"Droids," the guy said. And then nodded at Listic.

"Oh, good," Bek said under her breath.

"But I can't even drink anything!" Listic bobbed up and down in frustration. "Alan, tell him I can't even drink anything."

"It's okay, Listic," I said. "He's just kidding."

"Alan, I insist on going into this bar with you," Listic went on. "It's a matter of principle. I mean, how would you feel if—"

"Listic, Off." She dropped into my hand. "Sorry about that. Manic Virus."

The doorman nodded. "It happens."

We went in and looked around. The band played that stupid song that made me realize if I was a staff member in this place I'd probably beat my head against the counter until I passed out. I recognized a few of the animatronic aliens populating a few tables. There were only a few actual USS Mickey passengers. And only one entrance. We'd be able to tell if old steely eyes marched in.

That's when I spotted an empty seat. But not just any empty seat. I nudged Bek with my elbow and nodded toward it.

"Oh my god. It's available?"

"Hurry, before anyone takes it!"

We rushed over to The Booth. I sat where Han sat, she said where Greedo sat. I felt giddy as a child.

"So what are your thoughts on the matter?" she asked.

"Han shot first."

She nodded whole-heartedly.

A waiter wearing desert garb and a name badge with mouse ears, "Earl," came over and took our order. A coke for me, a whiskey and coke for her. I reactivated Listic, acknowledged I understood her plight regarding droid rights, then suggested maybe we could save that conversation for another day, and really, I'd appreciate it if she could keep an eye out by the entrance for the assassin. Having renewed purpose, she obliged.

"So," I said.

"I'm surprised they didn't keep me from coming in," she said. "You know, being an android, and all."

The waiter brought us our drinks.

"We both know that's not true," I said.

"That's just it, Alan. I don't know. Seriously, this makes no sense to me." She took a swig.

I looked at her drink. Curious. "Can you actually taste that?"

She shrugged. "Hardly. It's more like it's... filtered through a sensate matrix, or something? Like, I know it's whiskey and coke, but it doesn't taste like whiskey and coke. Kind of like you can see the color red, but not feel the color red. But you know red is red. And you can tell red from blue, but if you had to describe the difference between red and blue to a person who's been blind from birth, you couldn't. Trying to describe color is almost like acknowledging that color doesn't exist, or that it's superficial. It's kind of like that. I know what this drink is, I can tell what it is, but I have no actual sense of taste. No flavor."

"So when I first encountered you. The coffee..."

"That's when I found out. That I could't taste things the same way. It was disturbing, I admit. But I found the act of making the coffee, drinking the coffee, calming. Whatever I can do to feel normal, I'll take it." Her eyes expressed a sense of longing. A sense of loss. "Chocolate. I loved chocolate. I'd buy boxes of it, entire boxes just for myself—devour it when I was happy, binge on it when I was sad. Won't miss the sugar crashes, but still... chocolate."

"What about your sense of touch?"

"Same thing. Like I said on your bike, I could barely feel the wind on my face. It's like reading a dashboard. I can tell when I'm touching something, but I don't really feel it. God, it's so hard to explain. Oh! But that simulation? When we had to make the sandwiches?"

"Yeah?"

"Every time I grabbed the bread, I felt it. Like, that was really me touching the bread. Sure, it was a three year old version of me. But it was me, you know? Not like this." She knocked on her skull with her fist. "This is like being half dead, or something. Like, an orgasm would be nothing more than all the needles on my dashboard maxing out."

I leaned back on the bench. "Well that sucks."

"You're telling me!"

We sat there for a few moments, contemplating orgasms. At least, I assumed she was also contemplating orgasms. Once orgasms come up in a conversation, it kind of sticks. Needed to give it a moment. I twisted my soda glass in a circle while sweat dripped from its walls and pooled on the table. When I felt like enough time went by, I ventured a new topic.

"Speaking of telling me things... You still haven't told me about the last thing you remember before waking up in The Boneyard. Aside that you were 'running,' which induces a deal of curiosity."

She shrugged and swirled her drink around. "It seems so unimportant now. I mean, since then? Let's see... Well, I killed a man, so there's that. I woke up on a planet I've never heard of. And somehow, I'm a robot, now. What else? Oh, I'm being chased by an assassin. And I'm like a hundred and sixty years old. Everyone I know? Dead. Genocide by time travel."

"When you put it that way..."

"Yeah! It's pretty fucked up. So this whole thing about where I was last, and what I was doing there... Who cares." She wiped her eyes while I waited a beat. I knew she'd get there, she just needed to vent. She took a deep breath and continued to talk while staring at her drink. "Three days ago, by my recollection, I was on the verge of a landmark anthropological discovery on an as yet unexplored planet."

"Really."

"Really. But for all I know? Somebody else's discovered it since then, and the planet's been fully colonized. Three days turned out to be a hundred and thirty years."

I sat back and waited. She went on.

"My anthropology team—I keep calling them that, but I shouldn't. They're not all anthropologists. One of them's a linguist, another's a sociologist. Richard's even a theologist with a side hobby in geology. But you know what I mean… We were doing an excavation on a planet nearly as far out as you could go. It was an Edgeworld, but for all I know, it's been incorporated into one of the Clusters by now. That's the thing about the Edge."

"It's always moving further out."

"Right." She nodded and took another swig. "So we'd honed in on this particular planet because Richard noticed something unusual. Something from an orbital telescope. The scope had captured an image of a crater on this desolate rock that looked as though it had a human-made underground entrance. Like a subway entrance, leading into the heart of the planet."

"That's strange," I agreed. "And you were sure it wasn't a regular cave? Like a natural formation?"

"Oh, it was a cave, alright. But it was decidedly unnatural. That was all Richard. He gave us a PowerPoint presentation on it. They still use PowerPoint 3D?"

"Unfortunately."

"He had these holographic slides showing how meteors create craters, and how craters were sure to erode around their rims over eons, and that all lined up. Natural phenomenon. But there was no way this particular formation would have formed naturally at the crater's point of impact. It could only exist due to intelligent design. On a planet humans had yet to explore."

"Okay, that's freaky."

"Freaky weird for most people. Freaky awesome if you're an extra terrestrial anthropologist. Life on other planets, Alan. That's what we thought we'd discovered."

I nodded. The animatronic band started playing the obnoxious Cantina song again.

"So we applied for a bullshit grant, asking for funds to explore that planet on account of its potential geological resources. I can't even remember everything we claimed we'd be doing on the expedition, but that wasn't my part of the thing. Eddie, the astrophysicist, we left the grant writing up to him. Richard was so sure of this alien construct thing, he told us not to worry about it. If we didn't follow through with using our funding appropriately, all would be forgiven as soon as we informed our fellow humans we weren't, as it turns out, the only intelligent life in the galaxy. And he was right."

I leaned forward. "You found other life?"

"Almost," Bek said. She looked around to make sure no one was listening to our conversation, then leaned in and whispered. "We discovered a dead civilization."

"What?"

"Seriously. I know, it's hard to believe. But beneath the surface of the planet? It was like Journey to the Center of the Earth down there. The Land That Time Forgot, The Lost World, The Genesis Project. Whatever. It was a jungle down there. A literal, breathing jungle, below the surface of the planet, with phosphorescent stalactites and glowing moss. An entire ecosystem."

"Like a terradome."

"Like a terradome. But that wasn't the craziest part. Not even. The craziest part?" She swallowed. "We found a temple down there. No aliens, but an ancient temple. Mother Nature doesn't sculpt staircases like that. Let alone what we found inside."

I sat back again, took a drink of my soda. "That's a lot to digest."

"Try digesting all that, and then waking up at The Boneyard."

I could only imagine. "And the last thing? What's the last thing you remember. Before The Boneyard."

"Being chased." She shifted in her seat. "I admit, that's the part I probably should have shared with you already. I'm not sure if it has anything to do with that intense guy following us around now, but my anthro team was raided. Whoever they were, they'd followed us to the planet and snuck into the temple we'd set up camp in. Richard, he..." She swallowed and took a deep breath. "He was shot, right before my eyes. The last thing I remember was Eddie grabbing my wrist and pulling me down a tunnel. Janson—he was the linguist—I heard Janson trying to reason with them, but then I heard another gunshot, and I didn't hear Janson anymore. And that's it! There's no 'last moment' I can recall. The whole memory fades out at that point. Like... Like you know how you can't recall the exact moment you fell asleep at night? You can remember waking up, the actual moment you wake up is vivid enough. But you can never remember the exact moment you fell asleep. It's like that. It's like, at some point while I was running through a tunnel with Eddie, I just... fell asleep."

My gut was telling me something. Pieces were coming together, I could feel it. Only I still didn't know what the big picture was. Not yet. "I realize you don't want anyone to know this, but: Where is this planet?"

"I couldn't tell you."

"Bek, you can trust me. You know that, right?"

"No, I mean I literally couldn't tell you. I have no idea. Eddie could. Perhaps even Richard. But that wasn't my part of the gig. I was more interested in what was on the planet, not so much where the planet was. I'm no astrophysicist, let alone an astronomer. Hell, I could hardly even recognize the constellations from my home world's point of view. Hank was always looking up at the night sky like, 'That one's Utah,' or 'That one's Florida,' but I could never tell."

"Your home planet's starscape constellations were named after Earth's United States of America?"

"We weren't very original." She finished off her whiskey and coke. "My sensate matrix, or whatever, informs me this drink was light on the whiskey. Not that it matters. I don't think I could get my android brain drunk if I wanted to."

"Don't give up yet, Bek."

"You think I should order another one?"

"No, I mean don't give up on finding out what happened. I have a feeling we'll find something at the Scrappery."

"We're still doing it? Despite that guy's cocktail note from hell?"

I finished off my drink and leaned forward. "Are you kidding? That cocktail note only made me want to do the opposite."

She smiled. "Works for me. You only live once." She looked down at her own body and fanned out her arms. "Or twice."

14

Dark Alley

We passed on the Sarlacc Pit, as it was too easy to imagine getting tossed into it by a hidden assassin. But we'd be fools to pass on the Build Your Own Lightsaber vending machine.

The build involved answering a twenty-eight question survey. I wanted to end up with a purple lightsaber—or "amethyst," as Bek kept insisting—so it was difficult to answer the questions without wondering how Mace Windu would answer them. Every time I wanted to respond like a serious badass, my finger hovering over the touch screen, Bek would chime in with, "Now remember, answer honestly." Totally killed my chances. I ended up with a blue one, while Bek ended up with green.

"Wow, that machine knows its shit," Bek said. We were walking back to our rooms, down the mahogany corridor, as she waved her saber around in front of her. The beam was a holographic projection, of course—vibrant and bright and humming in sync with her slices, but not at all tangible, the laws of physics being what they were these days in a galaxy close, close by.

"So you're Yoda, are you?" I tried to keep the jealousy out of my voice, but even I picked up on it.

"Luke," she said. "Refashioned."

"Huh," I reflected. "You're right, that machine does know its shit."

Listic was scouting ahead, but I knew it didn't count for much. To be honest, I didn't think the assassin was following us anymore. He probably thought he'd scared us shitless with his ambiguous napkin threat. Little did he know he was now dealing with two newly minted Jedi. As ridiculous as it seemed, there was something about holding holographic toys that made us feel more secure.

The games we play with ourselves, even into adulthood. Bike helmets, seat belts, door locks, side arms... These were all bet-hedgers for specific scenarios you would most likely never encounter. Even then, bike helmets cracked, seat belts strangled, door locks busted, side arms backfired. In truth, when your time comes, it comes. No one lives forever, and it was nothing short of faith that kept people from freaking out about their imminent death every single day. Faith in a god, a spirit, an idol, a weapon... Faith that maybe you'll be the first person ever who doesn't actually die. So if the false security of a toy lightsaber helps, I'll take it. It was as real as any of it.

Even so, my useless trail of thoughts led to some practicality. I thought of a way we might use our new tools to our advantage. I explained it to Bek after we'd gotten back into our closet and locked its sailor duck door.

"Alan, that's gotta be the dumbest idea I've ever heard." But she said it with a half-smile.

"That's what I'm good at," I said. "Dumb ideas that somehow manage to work."

· • ·

Bek and I exited the USS Mickey along with the ship's other passengers via the space station's airlock tube that funneled us into the terminal. Immediately to the left and right of the terminal was the casino, and somewhere beyond the casino was the Scrappery. I looked to the right and saw brightly lit gaming holographs dotting an otherwise darkened ring that gradually curved toward a distant vanishing point.

We had a lot of ring to cover.

Listic went zipping off into the crowd. Tall, dark, and handsome was already in the middle of the terminal chaos, casually leaning against a pillar twenty feet away, watching us disembark. He made eye contact with me, then nodded toward the ticket station. I looked in that direction and discovered the next flight back, the USS Donald, departed in a little over an hour, whereas the USS Mickey wouldn't be heading back for two days. The assassin expected us terrified, terminally hunted prey to turn tail and take the Donald the hell out of here.

I looked straight at steely eyes and offered him the most exquisite bird I have ever flipped in my life. This thing was majestic. My index and ring fingers sat perfectly balanced on both sides of my fully erect middle finger. And I held it there, solid as stone, for a three-count.

He shrugged and wandered back into the crowd. It was on.

We did not head to the ticket station. We headed toward the casino entrance on the right. Baccarin's Palace.

"Okay, remember the plan," I said in a low voice.

"Got it."

"You sure?"

"It's not a difficult plan, Alan," Bek said. "It's 'You go one way, and I'll go the other.'"

I nodded. "Okay, you got it." We passed beneath the holographic golden gleam of the casino sign and into an unending network of gambling devices. There was no light from the ceiling, only light from machines and tables, holoboards and holograms. It was hard on my eyes at first, but after a minute, the setting proved both mesmerizing and evocative.

I felt pulled into the ordered chaos, like some part of my being was being tugged on and fucked with. It was like taking the first bite of a crackdog and then suddenly realizing how hungry you were. One crackdog always led to another, just like one goola gambled led to another. The only difference was, after so many crackdogs, you were stuffed, whereas after so many goola, you were emptied. Either way, you looked back and saw yourself the fool.

To my right were a dozen people watching a holoboard with baited breath. The board projected a wagered game, two teams competing against each other for domination over a fantasy kingdom. Dragon breath flared and wizard bolts crackled above everyone's heads as camera angles danced a choreography of bloodshed. A red knight fell and half the crowd cheered while the other half booed. A blue elf exploded, resulting in an inverse response.

I'd heard about these games. Red verses Blue, avatar teams of various fictions vying over control of realms or galaxies. Hundreds of years ago, actual people controlled the avatars in what were called video games. But once AIs became standard, the avatars became computer driven. These people were betting on computers pretending to be computers, teams of pixelated icons, legioned and personified.

Looking across the room, I took in an entire hall filled with elaborate variations of rock, paper, scissors. Glowing podiums players tapped in random places. Decks of cards floating above counters. Glowing balls bouncing into guttered numbers. Their complexity lured participants into a false sense of control, a belief they could outsmart the odds. But in reality, the games were all roshambo with flair.

I forced my eyes elsewhere, looked for dark nooks in the room—a difficult task, being the photo negative of what the casino architects guided your eyes towards. Yet perfect, for that very reason.

I spotted two such alcoves. One to my right, not far beyond the fantasy game monitor, dark in contrast to its surrounding attractions. The other to Bek's left, an offshoot to some staff-only area.

"There," I said without pointing. "You see that gap along the wall? Behind Mighty Mike's Grip of Goola machine?"

"The dark narrow hallway leading straight to imminent death?"

"Yes, that one. That one's yours. I'm heading for the abyss of darkness to the right."

"Have fun." We started heading in opposite directions when she stopped and turned back to me. "Hey, Alan?"

"Yeah?"

"If we don't make it through this…" She swallowed. "I want you to know…" I swallowed. "My green lightsaber is way better than your blue lightsaber." She made a childish face—the classic stick-your-tongue-out-and-cross-your-eyes face—and left.

I wormed through the crowd of gamblers and distanced myself from the bling and the blare, then did my best to make myself look vulnerable. This turned out to be easy, since right at that moment, my quarkphone rang, making me actually vulnerable. Of all the times for Alice to call.

Of course, I had to take it.

"Alice, now's not the—"

"Alan, I looked into that serial number you gave me. It's in the system."

"Can I call you back in—wait, it is?"

"It is. I was searching the wrong data base, though. You had me chasing a red herring."

"What do you mean, a red herring?"

"You don't know what a red herring is? I learned about it in class yesterday. It's like a false lead. It's a device—"

"No, I know what a—"

"—used in crime fiction, like when the author wants to mislead the reader, but it can happen in—"

"Alice, I know what a red herring is, alright? I mean in what way was it a red herring?"

"Oh. Yeah, that makes sense. Okay, so it's not a serial number for an ORB. It's not a serial number, at all. It's—"

Something brushed my jacket's collar on its way to chopping my neck.

"Christ!" I went spilling to the ground while the blow jackknifed my head into my shoulder. My quarkphone flew out of my hand and landed ten feet away, breaking into at least two pieces. It looked like I was the lucky winner of the Assassin's First Choice Award.

"Couldn't just turn around and head back, could you, Alan Blades?" His voice was as steely as his eyes. "You know, I've been given strict orders to let you live. Idea's been to scare the shit out of you. But I don't take kindly to being flipped off. And accidents do happen."

I massaged my neck with one hand while slowly reaching behind my back with the other. "So you're going to kill me. Because I flipped you off. Have you heard of the term 'overreaction?'"

He smiled. "I can't believe you thought I'd go after the girl. Such an obvious set up. What a ridiculous plan."

I stretched my neck out a bit, tried to work out the kink. "That wasn't the plan."

"Oh?" he seemed amused. He knew he could kill me in a heartbeat. At this point, he was playing with his prey. "So you knew I'd come for you first? You expect me to believe that?"

"Didn't matter who you came after first," I said. "Either way? This was going to happen." I whipped out my dormant lightsaber handle and grasped it with both hands.

He laughed. "You've gotta be kidding. You plan on taking me down with a toy?"

I surreptitiously tapped a button on my wristscreen, making it look like I was fumbling with my lightsaber's switch as it flared to life, bright and blue.

He took a fighting stance, almost curiously. If he lunged at me too soon, it would all be over. "What, you thought the light would blind me? I've got news for you, Blades. Permanent ORB implants. I can see just fine." He brought a fist back to plow into my skull.

Listic smacked him upside the head like a dull bullet, and the asshole tumbled to the ground. Out cold.

I switched off my lightsaber looked at my wristscreen. It read "Knock-Out Button Activated." Now THAT was a button.

"You okay?" I asked Listic as I stood up.

"Alan!" she said excitedly.

"Yeah?"

"Alan!"

"What?"

"We have GOT to do that more often!"

I propped the assassin up against the pipe.

Bek came running over. "You got him?"

"We got him. But he could have nanobot healers. I'm under the impression he's enhanced. Could come to any second. Care to kick in some insurance?"

Bek put on a tough expression as she looked at the debilitated threat. "Boy, would I."

"Commence."

She decked him with two right jabs and a left hook. Android strength. He would not be waking up for quite some time.

"Nice. Hold on, I want to search him." I patted down his designer wear and came up with two items: A quarkphone and a lightsaber handle.

"You're kidding," Bek said. "He's a Star Wars fan?"

I lit up his blade, expecting it to be red. But it wasn't. "He got purple?" Like I didn't already hate this guy enough.

"Amethyst." Bek insisted, but then realized she had just poured salt in my wound. "Sorry."

I flicked off the saber, opened his quarkphone, and saw incomings from only one person. The name made my stomach churn. They were all from Gina.

"What is it, Alan?" Bek could see the shock on my face. "Does that name mean something to you?"

I hit the call back button. The phone fizzled out and shut down, smoke spewing out of its underside, suddenly hot. "Crap!" I dropped it and it snapped in half. I was creating a quarkphone graveyard.

Bek's face went from curious to incredulous. "What the hell, man?"

"It must have been spliced to his signature. Anyone else trying to use it would cause it to self-destruct."

She took a deep breath. "Like in the Mission Impossible movies."

"Like in the Mission Impossible movies." I shook my hand and blew on my fingers.

"Who's Gina."

"My ex-partner."

"Ex-partner. As in, ex-wife?"

"No, as in ex-GalactiCop partner. Now she's part of CyberOps. Which means this guy must be part of CyberOps."

"What's a CyberOps?"

I shrugged. "Whatever they need to be. Covert espionage team. They were an offshoot of Fleet, but lately it seems like they act on their own with impunity."

Bek looked around to make sure nobody else was approaching us. "Good impunity or bad impunity?"

Good question. The seemingly random message I'd gotten from Gina on my own quarkphone scrolled through my head: DO NOT FOLLOW TRANSMISSION. REMAIN ON PLANET.

What the hell?

"I trust Gina with my life. But I'm beginning to wonder about the outfit she works for. I couldn't tell you what their angle is, these days." I latched the toy back onto the asshole's belt. "Okay, let's get Mace Windu back to the starcruiser."

"What, you're not keeping his lightsaber?"

"Never take another man's lightsaber," I said. Bek nodded in profound agreement. Ethics.

We propped him up and dragged his unconscious body back to the Mickey. It took the the two of us, and I was glad for Bek's android strength. The guy weighed a ton. Like Gina, he was probably loaded with cybernetics of the imperceptible variety. Unlike the bearded ballerina. The one he'd shot and killed.

Gina, what have you gotten yourself into?

Nobody in the casino even noticed us dragging him through the crowd, obsessed as they were with their wins and their losses. We wandered through the now empty terminal and made our way to Mickey's gate, told the crew member at the airlock our friend already had way too much gin and tonic at the Baccarin Casino, then drug him all the way to his passenger cabin. I lifted his braceleted wrist to activate his door, which was decorated with a minxy fairy, and slung him onto the padded bench.

"Computer," I said between heavy breaths to his cabin's VR station. "Activate simulation."

"Please select your age."

"Three years old."

A suction dart flew out of the wall and stuck to the assassin's forehead.

"Sweet dreams, asshole." I closed his door behind us. "Now. Let's find us a Scrappery."

15

Crappy Scrap

The Scrappery was on the opposite side of the space station's ring. As part of the FU Conglomerate, those who lived and/or did business there didn't have to abide by Standard Cluster Law. GalactiCops had no jurisdiction in that hemisphere. No one did. Much like the wasteland beyond Fillion's dome, it was a free for all, where derelicts of all sorts could barter and trade and scavenge and hide.

Bek and I wormed our way through the space station's casino and subsequent hotel area, a nearly endless stretch of room doors alternating with enticing gambling machines. I had to turn Listic off, as it was far too draining to tell her no, we don't have time to play that game right now, or no, I'm not feeding you any goola from my ethernet account, every ten seconds. Besides, I felt like we were in the clear for awhile as far at being trailed by tall, dark, and handsome. Eventually, through what amounted to sheer perseverance despite the well-honed marketing strategies gleaned from centuries of greedy capitalist practices, Bek and I wound up in a dead zone at the farthest end of the casino resort's tubescape. All the lights and bling and noise, all the vacant-eyed participants... It all died. The conduit turned into a barren pocket of cement and metal, a sterile zone of intimidation and fear. Four border guards stood around a force barrier, two to a side. I approached one with what I hoped came off as confidence rather than outright trepidation.

"State your business," he said.

Humphrey, the fatherly gatekeeper of the airlock back on Fillion, was a rare exception to the general rule. I found myself wondering if bullish assholes tended to become barrier guards, or if barrier guards tended to become bullish assholes. Functionalism at its finest. "We'd like to visit the Scrappery," I said. No point in lying.

"Where you from?"

"Fillion."

"Do you have any hazardous waste on you?"

"No."

"Any oranges? Citrus fruit of any kind?"

"What? No, no citrus fruit."

"Do you play any musical instruments?" They looked at Bek. "Either of you?"

I threw my hands out. "What does that have to do with—"

"Marv. He's looking for another banjo player. None of us play. He keeps bringing two banjos, like one of us is going to learn overnight and be all excited to play with him the next day."

Marv piped up with the kind of immediacy that betrayed an ongoing argument. "Or just pick up the damn thing and learn how to play while we're here! Christ sake, you guys are lazy..."

The first guard ignored him. "So either of you play banjo?"

"No. No, we don't play the banjo." I looked curiously over at Bek "Do we?"

"Actually?" Bek said. "I do. I play the banjo."

"You play the banjo."

She shrugged. "I grew up on a farm."

"Prove it," the first guard said.

"What, like a test to move on to the next area?" she said with an edge of excitement. "Oh! Like the organ in Goonies?"

"Such a great movie," I said.

"I know, right?"

"That Data kid, and those gadgets he—"

"Okay, enough," the guard interrupted. "I have no idea what a goonie is, but yes, it's a test. Do you play, or don't you?"

Bek swallowed hard. "Well, I mean, it's been awhile, but..."

One of the guards from the background walked forward holding two instrument cases. He unzipped one and handed a banjo to Bek. Unzipped the other, handed a banjo to Marv. Marv was beaming like you wouldn't believe. It was a holiday for Marv. It was Marvday. He waited patiently for Bek to tune her instrument, eyes gleaming with anticipation. And then, with utmost sincerity, he played the first refrain of dueling banjos.

Bek answered in kind. Before we knew it, the other three guards and I were tapping our feet and clapping, really yee-hawing it up. It was a musical tsunami, and trying to keep the good vibes at bay would have been like trying to hold back a tidal wave with your arms. Finally, the song came to a close, our tiny audience applauded, and a smiling Bek handed the banjo back to them while juggling the compliments that gushed out of everyone's mouths.

The first guard waved us toward the gate.

"That's it?" Bek asked. "We're allowed to go through, now?"

"Of course," he said. "Everyone's allowed through. We sure aren't going to stop you."

"Our job?" Marv said. "Is to keep those FUCs from coming out."

. . .

Bek and I walked along a wide corridor lined with beggars and outcasts, the glow of the force barrier fading in our wake. Some people were barely standing, others lying down and mumbling. Most were sitting against the walls, with that same vacant stare I'd seen gamblers wearing back in the casino, only these were entirely devoid of hope. Like Rutger and Howard, all of them had bowls or baskets laid out in front of them, and all their shallow vessels harbored but one or two goola chips—just enough to remind you of what the bowl was for, but not so many you didn't think they could use more.

Bad fluorescent lighting flickered overhead, allowing for glimpses of graffiti, rust, and refuse. The stink of the place made me consider surgically removing my olfactory senses as soon as possible. One poor girl, younger than the most, had a bandage wrapped around her jaw.

"This is a travesty," Bek said.

It was. I felt sick to my stomach. How was it okay to let people live in such squalor? They shared the same orbital ring, for god's sake. Right on the other side of that barrier, there were people disposing of disposable income. They were gambling goola on holographic roulette tables and old fashioned one-armed bandits. Literally throwing money away. And starcruisers kept dumping them out in mass. Meanwhile, this poor young girl couldn't afford to see a doctor. It didn't make any sense.

I pulled out a five-goola chip and dropped it in her bowl.

"Gee, thanks, mister," she said with watery eyes.

I nodded. "You know the way to the Scrappery?"

"Well gee whiz, sure I does." One of the boys next to her poked at her shoulder, but she flicked his hand away and kept talking. "All ya gotta do is keep walking in that direction." The boy tapped her shoulder again. Repeatedly. "Can't miss it if you—stop that, Henry!"

"It's my turn, Margaret. Let me wear it."

"You had it on all yesterday. I get a spell."

"But you're a girl. That right there's good enough. Look, I haven't earned a chip all day." He waved to his bowl. It had one chip in it. The starter chip.

"Oh, alright, here." She unwound the bandage from her head, talking to me again as she did so. "As. I. Was. Saying. You can't miss it. Huge buckets of parts. People all millin' about. It's a big production, it is."

The boy took the bandage from her and begin wrapping it around his head as though he'd rehearsed it a hundred times. He probably had.

I looked back down at her beggar's bowl. "You want your goola back, now?" she said with resignation.

"Of course not," I said. "You earned it."

"Well alright, then."

I gave her a pat on the head and reluctantly walked away.

We must have walked a quarter mile of conduit like that. For every goola I dropped, I felt guilty for not dropping more. I still had a lot of money in my ethernet account, but I ran out of chips in my pocket well before I made it to the end of the homeless gauntlet.

The hallway eventually opened up into an enormous hanger bay with a window spanning its curved perimeter. The bay must have been four times the size of the natural battle stadium at the base of Mt. Zelazny, populated with what amounted to fifty Hack Shacks. Space shuttles, ETUVs, portable buildings, wide tents... And between the vendors, in the haphazard aisles, were rivers of odd characters haggling over everything within reach. Even the merchants appeared to be customers, buying and selling and trading in a flurry of resales.

I looked along the inner arc of the massive bay and spotted a handful of corridors much like the one Bek and I had passed through. Each of the wide entrances had words painted above them in what looked like nothing less than blood. "Chop Shop," one of them read, and then in smaller letters beneath it, "Bought a part? Have it attached!" Another entrance said "Hallucinogenic Hall," another said "The Goola Laundry." I supposed there was no point in hiding the gateways to illegality in a place where nothing was illegal.

I looked up and behind me as we entered the fray to see what the hell our corridor was labeled. "Gambling and Buffet." And in smaller letters: "Bribe required at gate. No citrus."

We wandered into the din of material acquisition. Most of the vendors sold outdated, illegal cyberwear. Others sold random tech like hair dryers and toaster ovens—things like I'd find at Remy's. All of it was old and refurbished, or old and broken, or new and cheap and soon to be broken. None of it was new and of any quality.

"What a mess," I said. "How can people want this stuff?"

"Hey, look!" Bek said with glee. "That guy's selling movies!"

A droopy sign five lots further read "Bernie's Bootlegs." Having recently mastered navigating the dense crowds back at the casino, we reached him in a heartbeat.

"Buy two, get one free," Bernie said, lazily fanning himself with a laser disc jacket while sitting in a collapsible chair and looking out the wide bay window into deep space.

I glanced over at Bek, who was already rifling through the adventure section. "Something tells me that won't be a problem."

· · ·

We discovered twenty-six must-have movies between the two of us—which of course meant we ended up with twenty-seven, because of the whole units of "three" thing—before convincing each other to pull away. Like maybe we should stop shopping and go back to looking into the nature of Bek's existence, the entire purpose of our trip. We were lugging our bags of loot toward an ORB vendor we spotted further down when Bek stopped short. I didn't realize she'd fallen behind until I heard her voice, which sounded distant in more ways than one.

"I don't think I want to know anymore, Alan."

I turned around and looked at her. Her shoulders were sagging, in this case due to her mood rather than the movie bags. "Bek..." I considered making a joke about buyer's remorse, but then thought the better of it. She needed to talk this out. I waited for her to continue.

"Maybe I can just go on like this, you know? Recharging my battery rather than eating. Half-feeling, half-tasting. Half dead."

I found an opportunity to step closer to her among the ebb and flow of customers walking back and forth between the two of us. "Why would you want to do that?"

"Because maybe I'm not half dead. Maybe I'm all dead." She didn't make eye contact with me, kept staring off toward the ground. "It's like we talked about. Maybe this is all there is of me. Maybe the real me is dead." She looked at me. "Is that what we're doing, Alan? Trying to determine if I'm dead?"

"You know it's not."

"Then what? What is the point of all this?"

"We're trying to to determine if you're alive." I gave her a moment to process before going on. "Listen, Bek. This is your call. You hired me, right? I'm working for you. We don't have to keep moving forward on this."

"And do what, then? Go where? I'm still a wanted killer, aren't I? And I've gotten you involved as an accessory. And it's only a matter of time before that assassin catches back up with us. It's not like we can just turn around."

I thought about it. "Well, not directly around, perhaps. But there is a place we could go."

"Your island?"

"My island. There are flights to Victoria all the time. We might not want to go back through the casino to catch one, but I'm sure we could grab one from this side of the station. Most of these derelicts probably float further toward the Edge, but there are probably a significant number who float back in. That's how your ORB ended up on Fillion, after all." I gestured to the bay window, toward a collection of ships docked to a station pier. "I'm sure one them must be going to Victoria..."

"And do what? Live on an island?"

I shrugged. "It's possible. Sleep in sleeping bags, build campfires, live off fish and coconuts..."

"You could live off fish and coconuts, maybe. But unless your island has a power outlet? I'd crash, Alan. Not to mention... No power?" She lifted and lowered her bags. "No movies."

"Hey, I never said it would be easy..."

She slumped. "Oh, who are we fooling? That's no way to live." She shook her head and stood up straight again. "Thank you, but... We've come this far. I've never been a quitter, never shied away from the truth. I'm not going to start now." She walked past me toward the ORB vendor. "Let's get this over with."

I sighed with relief. I hated coconuts.

I walked ten final steps to reach a random knick-knack booth on a space station in the furthest reaches of known space in order to find out if a renegade sexbot was actually a human extraterrestrial anthropologist. Sometimes I reflected on having the damnedest of jobs. This was one of those times.

"Hello, miss," said the skinny, weaselly man behind the table. "Looking for something in particular? An ORB with a virus? One without? A tabula rasa? I have them all."

"I have one already," she tapped her temple, "but I'm hoping you can tell me more about it." She looked over at me. "God, I hate this part." She reached up to eject her eye from its socket. "Alan, if I forget what happened over the past couple hours, catch me back up to speed, okay? I trust—"

"Wait!" I said, grabbing her arm. "You might not have to do that again. I already know something about it."

She looked at me suspiciously. "What do you already know?"

"I know its serial number. I memorized it." I looked back at the weasel guy. "AX273472. That mean anything to you?"

He laughed. "Hey man, it's not like I keep a log of serial numbers on hand, right? Who would keep track of all the serial numbers of all the shit they sold? That'd be crazy."

Bek looked back and forth at the two of us, her hand still hovering next to her face. "So do I need to..."

"Fortunately for you?" Weasel said. "No. Cuz that's not a serial number."

"Well, what is it, then?" I asked.

"It's an ansible number."

"Of course it is," Bek said, defeated. She slowly lowered her hand.

"Like from a quarkphone," I said.

"Bingo," the vendor replied with the smile of someone who gets to explain things he thinks he knows more about than you. "The ol' 'intimacy ansible.' Yikes, what a disaster that was, huh? So many lawsuits. You have one of those, miss? They're tough to track down. I've only ever had one of them pass through my hands. In fact, it made me kind of a local celebrity in this joint, my fifteen microseconds of fame. I'm the only Scrappery vendor I know of who's bought and sold an IA."

I recalled Alice's number, Dan's Steak House number, and the few other ansible numbers I was familiar with from the contact list of my now departed quarkphone. Their alphanumeric signature was indeed similar, but... "I thought all ansible numbers started with a 1."

"They do, if they're open systems. Omniquarks. Anybody can call each other on those. But on a closed system, when two are exclusively synced to each other, you drop the 1." He looked at Bek. "You got a random sweetheart on the other end? Someone feeding into yours? Its counterpart might still be out there somewhere..."

"Yeah, I know exactly where its counterpart is," she said with a mixture of loss and distain. It was in her deceased ex-husband's skull.

The vendor wasn't quite sure how to handle her reaction. "Okay..."

Bek looked at me. "This gets us nowhere, Alan. We came all this way to learn something I already knew." She dropped her movie bags, sat on them, propped her chin up with her hands, and assumed what can only be described as a prime pouting position. "We might as well go back. I'll turn myself in at the GalactiCop station. Do androids go to prison? Or will they dismantle me?"

"Hang on." I looked back at the vendor. Something unlocked in my head. Like my brain finally processed what my gut's been telling me all along. "You mentioned only one of these IA ORBs ever passed through your hands..."

"Well, maybe two, now. You looking to sell, honey?"

"She's not looking to sell," I said on her behalf. Bek was out of it. "So do you have a record of who you bought it from?"

"I tell ya, you and your receipts and your serial numbers. Of course not. We don't run that way here—hurk!"

I grabbed the weasel by the scruff of his shirt and yanked him closer to me. Apparently this was a regular dynamic in the Scrappery, seeing as how no one nearby cared to notice. If the bearded ballerina recalled where he'd gotten one of these from... "Oh, come on. Only one of these ever passed through your hands and you can't remember where it came from?"

"B-but that's not to say I don't remember who sold it to me!" I let go. He leaned back and brushed off his shirt, then fanned his hand out to the table. "See anything here you like?"

Christ. "Sure. How much for this one?" I picked up the first ORB I touched.

"Fifty goola."

"I'll give you a hundred," I said. "You accept ethernet transfers?"

He cleared his throat and nodded.

I pocketed my latest ORB, a copper number with a green iris, touched my thumb against his GoolaPal screen and watched my account take a hit. "Okay. Spill."

"There's a scavenger ship, docks every few months, Scrapside." He gestured to the port gate on the outer wall past the wide window, toward the cluster of docked freighters on the station pier. "Bunch of scavengers who claim to only steal from dead zones. Like that makes it alright, you know? Although I suppose that's the very definition of a scavenger."

"As opposed to a raider," I responded. Back when I was a GalactiCop, we'd often look the other way when it came to scavengers. Even though looting ghost ships was illegal, it was a gray area, ethically speaking. Scavenging was the equivalent of a misdemeanor, since no one was directly harmed by the act. True, spoils were being stolen, albeit the postmortem nature of the crime lessened its severity. It was raiding and piracy we didn't turn a blind eye to, the former amounting to planet-based encounters, the latter space-based, but in either case, they involved threatening, enslaving, or killing others as part of the deed.

No one liked pirates. No one liked raiders. But scavengers, no one could care less about.

"Right," the vendor said. "So the scavengers, they found this dead raider ship, right? Recognized it as a raider ship by its register code. Had a bounty on it from like a hundred years ago. They boarded it and wound up with the IA-ORB, not to mention a bunch of old science equipment. Anyway, their ship, the scavenger's ship, it's called the Roach. Looks like one, too. I bought the ORB offa them. "

My gut was churning with clue glue at this point. "You sure?"

"Hey, like you said. It's my business to know. Literally. I even remember them telling me where they found it. The raider ship. It was orbiting a planet further out on the Edge. Don't know the name of the planet, though." He swallowed hard. "Swear to god."

"Thanks." I nodded. "Sorry about the, you know... The throat grab."

"Don't mention it."

"Every few months, huh? So when are they due back?"

"Well, they were already here a couple of weeks ago, so..."

Dammit! If they only came every few months, it would be too long before they returned. What were Bek and I supposed to do now? Pay the bribe at the casino barrier, grab a hotel room, and avoid an assassin for another couple months? Wait it out in beggar's row with a goola bowl between us? Why did it always seem like I was one step away from getting somewhere only to have it pulled out from under me?

He went on. "...So it's a little odd they showed up again so soon."

My heart lightened. "What, they're here now?"

"Someone's lucky day, I guess."

I reached across the table again. He flinched, but quickly softened when my hand landed on his shoulder rather than his throat. "Thank you."

"Yeah, sure, man. Whatever."

"Bek, get up. We need to go."

She sat there with her chin on her hands, looking depressed. "Oh, what's the point, Alan." A statement, not a question. Hadn't she heard any of this? Was she that out of it?

"C'mon, get up!" I grabbed her wrists and pulled her up. She slowly pivoted and picked up her movie bags, then let me lead her toward the gate.

"I honestly don't see what the big deal is. You think because some scavengers traded some ORB like mine to some guy here, those scavengers are going to lead us to another stupid clue about me?"

"Bek? That ORB he bought from them?"

"Yeah?"

"It wasn't one like yours."

She shook her head. "But I thought he said—"

"No, the ORB he bought wasn't like yours. It was yours."

She looked to the floor and thought about it for a second. "Oh." Then she looked straight at me. "Oh! Of course! That raider ship, it had a bounty on it from over a hundred years ago. The old science equipment the scavengers found on it... The ORB they found on it... Oh my god, Alan. It was them! They were the raiders that attacked the planet my anthro team was on."

"So you were listening after all."

"And that could mean the planet their ship was orbiting..." She took in a quick breath, the way a child would when offered a surprise birthday gift. "That planet might be mine! I mean, maybe not. Maybe the raiders left and ended up orbiting a different planet. But there's a chance, right Alan? There's a chance they never left after they raided us. That could be the planet my team discovered!"

"Bingo." I cleared my throat. "But even if it isn't—"

"Don't say that."

"But even if it isn't, if we can find that ship, we can look at its flight records. We can determine where it's been."

Bek nodded, resolute. She walked right past me toward the port gate. I scrambled to catch up. We had another lead to follow. But I found myself questioning my own motivation at this point. Was I following a lead?

Or was I following Bek?

16

Flying Roaches

The good news was, the crew of the Roach was packing up to depart. The bad news was, they weren't going the direction we were hoping they'd go.

"Listen, Mr. Blades," said the burly ship captain with scars all over his face. "Been there, done that. We've got no reason to visit that hunk of rock again. Anything that system had to offer, we already unloaded it from that raider ship."

He flung another bag of cords and wires onto the bed of their orange hover-pallet truck thing.

"Boss is right," said a four-foot-tall woman with a skyscraper of a topknot while she took inventory on an old handheld multipurpose unit. "We've got other places to go."

"You can fly with us to Torres," Captain Scar said. "For four-thousand goola."

"We don't need to get to Torres," I said. "We need to get to… What was that planet called, again?"

"Tudyk," he replied. "The one with the raider ship was Tudyk."

I looked at Bek. She shrugged, as if to say "go with it." The planet didn't have a name back when she'd landed on it.

The captain went on. "You know, Tudyk. Like from Firefly? Like all the other planets around here?"

"What's a Firefly?" I asked.

"It was a show. Like all those movie discs you've got. One of the Edgeworld's astro-cartographers, huge Browncoat fan like me and my crew, named a lot of these planets after the cast." He nodded toward our bags of PDUs. "Don't you watch any of those movies you buy?"

Fighting words if ever there were. "Do I watch these? Of course I watch these. Just because I haven't seen all the same shows you have doesn't mean—"

"Of course!" Bek interrupted. Which was probably a good thing, as my wounded pride was going to blossom into full-blown ego defense. "Firefly! I thought 'Fillion' sounded familiar. That was the actor's name. Nathan Fillion."

"We've got us a fan!" Captain Scar said.

"Wait, you know this show?" I asked Bek. First the banjo, now this.

"You'd like it," Bek insisted.

The captain smirked. "You should check it out sometime, all I'm saying. Firefly. One of the greats. Prematurely cancelled."

"Cancelled," I repeated. "What, like hundreds of years ago?"

"We still haven't gotten over it," the captain replied gravely. Bek and the short topknot woman nodded with equal sincerity. He grabbed a second bag of wires but paused before tossing it on the pallet. "Hang on... You don't even know the name of this planet, and you want to go there? What do you know about it we don't?"

I didn't quite know how to respond to that one. Thankfully, Bek had us covered.

"My father," she said. "He... He was a planet raider. A crew member on that dead ship you discovered. Not the best person, I know. I know that much. But I hardly knew him at all, having gotten separated when I was only eight years old. And he, well... He was my father, right? I learned he died on that planet. I need closure, is all."

Wow. That was pretty good.

"Your father crewed that ship we scavenged?" He looked skeptical of her explanation. "Well, for the record, when we found it, there was no one on board. We ain't pirates, after all. We don't take what belongs to others, only what's left unclaimed. But I don't know... You're a young lady, and that ship seemed awfully old. At least a century, I'd argue. Wasn't even worth dismantling for parts, which was why all we took were the supplies we found on board..."

Bek didn't miss a beat. "It was old. I gave him a hard time about that, even as a little girl. The thing was a piece of junk, spent well past its commission. Was handed down from crew to crew, generation to generation. But his generation was the last. Now it circles the planet, empty and abandoned. And I don't even want the ship. Good riddance to the ship. I want to visit the site where my father died."

Captain Scar looked as though he believed her by then. His shoulders sagged a bit and his eyes went soft.

But then he stiffened again as though reacquainting with his original resolve. "Humph. Family. Take it from me, miss. Fuck 'em." He tossed the second bag onto the pallet.

"C'mon, help us out," I said.

"Torres. Four-thousand goola."

"We don't need to go to Torres. Listen, how much would it cost to change your mind?"

I gave him a ninety-percent chance to tell us to go fuck ourselves, but the little topknot slapped the back of her left hand against his chest while continuing to punch in some numbers with her right hand. "Wait." She hit a final button, then looked up at me. "A hundred-thousand goola. Take it or leave it." She looked over at Bek. "Not a bad deal, for closure."

I looked at the captain. He laughed. "Well, sure. For a hundred-thousand goola, I'll fly you to fucking Earth. You have a hundred-thousand goola? Didn't think so." He tumbled into the cab of the hover-pallet and grabbed the wheel.

"Hold on," I said. "Okay, so I don't have a hundred-thousand goola. Exactly. But I have this." I held out my hand for Topknot's multipurpose unit. She passed it up to me. I hit Assets and thumbed the screenreader. It acknowledged my I/DNA and brought up my accounts. With all this trip had cost me so far, I barely had enough left to cover rent next month. I thought of Marple and shivered. Don't worry, Alan, you'll make it work. Always do.

I scrolled down to my real estate bar. Thumbed it. Up popped my island. I handed the device back to Topknot.

"All yours, if you take us to Tudyk." I clarified. "Well, half of it, anyway. My ex-wife's sister owns the other half. Long story. Listen, I have no idea what she has planned for it, so you can't blame me if she builds a resort. But you can have my half."

I'd never seen eyes open so wide. Topknot's jaw literally dropped. "It's listed at fifty million goola," she said, barely, with what little breath she had left in her lungs.

"What?" The captain looked incredulous. "You must be reading it wrong. Let me see that." He yanked it from her.

"Oh, Alan," Bek said. "No, you can't. That's too much. No. No no no no no—"

"Works for me," he said, passing the device back to me. "Thumb the send key, we'll get you there in record time. Maximum burn."

I looked at Bek. "Listen to me. That island? It means nothing to me. It means washing out. It means letting life pass me by. It means not giving a damn."

"But Alan—"

"And I got too good at that, at not giving a damn. As soon as I was given that property, it was the last place I wanted to be. I want to be wherever the case takes me. And right now? It's taking me to Tudyk." I hit the send key.

The captain grabbed the device again and looked at the screen with an anxiety that quickly converted to elation. He then looked over at Topknot and nodded. Topknot slapped her hand to her forehead in euphoric disbelief.

"I... I can't believe you did that," Bek said. "You must really," she let out a short, nervous laugh, "hate coconuts."

"They're awful," I agreed. "Flavored water with flavorless pulp? They've totally got it backwards."

"Oh, Alan..."

"Alright, you crazy idiots," Captain Scar said. "All aboard."

We tossed our movie bags onto his hover-pallet and boarded the Roach.

· ● ·

Never has a ship had a more appropriate name than the Roach. It looked like one on the outside, and it was teeming with them on the inside. Not as bad as an Indiana Jones snake pit teemed with snakes, but still, it was bad. Shine a flashlight into any dark corner, and you'd hear scurrying. And hissing. These were the kinds of cockroaches that hissed.

The five of us—amounting to Bek and myself, the recently acquainted Captain Scar and Topknot, and a final crew member I mentally nicknamed "Shifty"—were circled around an old flatscreen monitor in the ship's dank, dark, and dismal communal quarters. Each of us had sunk into what they called beanbag chairs, these odd mounds of beans and pleather that conformed to our asses. I found them novel and comfortable at first, but after an hour, I started to feel sore all over. We'd been on the ship for two days—the first two of five in route to Tudyk—and we'd "binge watched" this Firefly show of theirs for the majority of our waking hours.

I wasn't used to this. I rarely watched serial episodes for this reason—it was nearly impossible to pull away. And the beanbag chairs weren't helping. Getting up was a physically monumental feat. At this point, my back was rebelling and my ass had entered a new dimension of numbness. But this show? Worth it.

The fourteenth episode came to a close.

"Wait, that's it?" I asked.

"That's it," Shifty said. "Show got cancelled after that."

I was dumbfounded. "But it didn't end. It wasn't over." Anger welled up inside of me. "Why the fuck would anyone cancel that show?"

"No one knows," Topknot said with a shrug. She stretched her arms up and worked out a kink in her neck by turning it as far as it would go to the right. They were over it by now, the show being cancelled, but I could tell they were getting off on how incredulous I'd become. Even Bek exhibited a melancholy smile as she looked over at me. Misery loves company.

Topknot went on. "There are a number of theories, but the true reason has been lost over time. Some say the production crew died. Others insist the warehouse in which the show was filmed was destroyed in a fire. It's still a mystery."

Listic piped up. "Actually, if you tap the Archives, you will learn the real reason involves a few incompetent produ—"

"Hold it!" Scar put his hand up and Listic stopped short. "Some things are better left unsaid. It is too devastating to think such a thing could have transpired on purpose."

"Oh, whatever, you guys," Shifty said. "Enough messing with the new guy, you all know why it ended. It was poorly promoted, they gave it a Friday night time slot, they aired the episodes out of order..."

"But..." I shook my head. "Why would they air the episodes out of order? Were they trying to fail?"

"Like my First Mate said," Scar's voice was solemn and true. "Parts of it really are a mystery. Keep in mind, this was back on Earth, twenty-first century—as in early twenty-first century, before the Cluster Migration. Pollution and all, they probably weren't thinking clearly. But in truth, who can fully comprehend the mind of a television executive?"

Everyone took a deep breath and stared into the void. Listic's eye dimmed. I had never experienced a moment of such shared and profound grief.

Shifty eventually rolled up from his beanbag with an ease I didn't know humanly possible. Apparently their bodies had become immune to the perpetual disfigurement these chairs imposed on their users. Either that, or they were already disfigured enough. This was the oddest looking crew I'd ever encountered. He went over to the DVD player and ejected the disc. "Should I tell him?" he asked.

"Tell me what?" I hated not being in on the joke.

Captain Scar got up and walked over to the communal room console that linked to the bridge, casually checked a few displays. "Sure."

"There's a movie," Bek said with glee, apparently fully aware of their secret. "The Browncoats united, insisted on closure. Funded a movie to put a cap on the whole thing."

I let out a deep breath I didn't realize I'd been holding. "Oh, thank god."

"It ain't perfect," Topknot said. "But it helps."

"It helps," Bek agreed. And they all nodded. Glory to god, amen.

Captain Scar cut a path through the room and headed toward the bridge.

"We'll save it for tomorrow. I need to check a few things on the upper deck. And you two need to—"

"Deal with the sludge," Topknot finished. "Yeah, yeah. Like we haven't been doing this for seven years."

"Deal with the sludge?" Bek asked. "What is the sludge?"

"This jalopy only has one mithrite conduit. It's attached to an accordion pipe that connects to the fusion inhibitor. Which is fine, normally. But as the sediment builds, we need to seal it, reconnect it to the exhaust port, and let out the refuse."

"Sounds complicated," Bek said.

Shifty slipped the disc into the DVD box jacket. "The Roach needs to take a shit." He looked at her and smiled, his pencil mustache accenting his face's unusual contortion. "Wanna help?"

Bek looked at me, then over at them. "I think we'll pass?"

"Suit yourself."

The two of them headed aft, leaving Bek and me alone in the room.

She rapped her fingers on her beanbag chair. "You, ah... I mean, did you want to help them? I probably shouldn't have answered for the both of us. Maybe we should have offered."

"What, help change a spaceship's diaper? No thanks. Besides, they're making millions off this trip. I think we're covered."

"That's kind of how I felt."

A cockroach landed on Bek's beanbag. And I mean landed. Because it flew there.

"Eeeeeek!" She flinched and curled into a ball. "Get it off! Get it off!" I struggled to lean out of my bag of laziness, but it held me tight in its embrace. She shot up from her own like a sprinter out of her starter blocks, reminding me she had a robot body. Apparently I was the only one onboard suffering hip displacement at this juncture.

I finally managed to reach over and flick it. It landed... somewhere.

"Where'd it go?" she said, eyes darting. "Where'd it go? Oh god, is it in my hair?"

I rolled over to the right, placing all fours on the floor, and began the arduous procedure toward verticality.

"Alan! Is it in my hair?!"

Listic was zipping around in a frenzy, up and down, circling, zooming in and out. "Alan, you have to help her! I have no arms! I have no arms!"

"Hold on, hold on..." Eventually I turned around and found her standing right next to me, pointing the top of her head at my face. I combed through her hair with my hands. The mood slowly transitioned from angst to intimacy. A warm feeling came over me as my fingers flowed through lush, silky waves. The fact her hair was synthetic was lost on me. This was Bek. I was touching Bek.

She looked up at me with wanton eyes. The words came slow. "Did you... Um... Was there a..."

"Hmmm?" I closed in a few more inches. My hand was still on the back of her head.

"I mean... What were we..."

"There it is!" Topknot shouted from behind me. I had no idea she'd come back in the room. Her tower of hair floated past my peripheral vision, like a braided shark fin. "Thought I'd seen it in here. Told him so." She grabbed a giant hydroponic wrench leaning against the bulkhead, then looked knowingly back at us. "Carry on."

I tried to recover. "So yeah, you're clean." I examined the top of her head with a surgeon's care. "There are no roaches in your hair. None."

Topknot rolled her eyes. "Oh, get a room, you two." She slung the wrench over her shoulder and left.

Bek looked back at me. "We have one, you know. A room."

"We do," I answered. "If you want it first, like last night, I can hang with Listic out here while you get some rest. Or plug in. Or whatever."

"Oh no, that's alright. I'm hardly tired. Why don't you take it first, tonight? I'll stay out here and... And I'll read one of these old books they have." She grabbed an old, rotting brick of paginated wood from the shelf and mumbled its title. "The Complete Guide to the Hitchhiker's Guide to the Galaxy. Wait, does that even make any sense? The Complete Guide to... So it's a guide to a guide? I'm not understanding this..." She opened the book and thumbed through brittle, inked pages.

"I insist, you take the room first," I said.

"No really, I'm not even tired. You need to rest that old man body of yours," she looked up at me with a smile.

"Hey, who's old? You're, like, a hundred and sixty? A hundred and sixty-five?"

"Once a woman is over a hundred, she stops disclosing her age." She looked back down at the page.

I had to admit, I was tired. Who knew watching seven hours of television from a beanbag chair could be so draining? "Well, okay. I mean, if you're sure."

She nodded briskly, eyes glued to the book as she took a seat on a workbench stool near where the wrench had been.

That fucking wrench.

"Night, then," I offered.

"Night."

Listic floated next to me down the hall and proceeded to tell me the actual reasons Firefly was cancelled. I entered our tiny room with the narrow cot, compact pillow, and wool blanket. I laid down and stared at the ceiling while she went on, telling me of all the exploits of the cast after the show was cancelled. The part about Tudyk—the actor, not the planet—going on to do that show called The Con Man was interesting. I always enjoyed stories that had a meta quality to them. But for the most part, I didn't hear what she was prattling on about.

I was thinking about Bek. Not her unresolved origin. Not her android circumstance. Just her smile, and her laugh, and her little telltale fidgets. Just...

Bek.

A knock at the door brought me back to the room. "Listic, Off." She floated down to my hand and I casually laid her in her cradle on a crate at the foot of the bed. I opened the door.

"I saw another one," Bek said calmly. "Another bug."

"You better come in here, then."

"Yeah, that's what I was thinking. I was thinking there are fewer... fewer bugs in here, you know? Than out there. So if you don't mind, I'll just read my book in here while you—"

I grabbed her waist with my left hand, brought her close, and kissed her.

The door shut behind her. She tossed the book on the crate, pushed me onto the cot, and kissed the hell out of me right back.

· ● ·

"Truth?" Bek said as she twirled my hair with her index finger. She was lying next to me on the narrow cot, soft and warm and real.

"Sure."

"I never saw anymore roaches out there."

I laughed. "I didn't think so."

She smiled. "Well, you are a detective, Mr. Alan Blades. I guess nothing gets past you."

I thought about what we'd done. And the variety of ways we'd done it. "Bek, that was...

"I know."

I'd never felt so connected to someone in my life. But I was worried. "Were you able to... I mean, it seemed like you did. But could you really..."

"Many times."

"Even though what you said before? About how you couldn't fully taste or feel anything, since waking up as an android? You know, your 'sensate matrix.'"

"I can't explain it either. I don't know if it's because this sexdoll body has all the right equipment, or if it's something else, but all that?" She stopped playing with my hair and looked me in the eyes. "I felt it, alright."

She reached for her book, grabbed it, set it on my chest, opened it. "I'm going to read for awhile. You rest." She smiled. "You earned it."

"Well, now that my male ego has been sufficiently placated, I suppose that is acceptable." I closed my eyes. She thumbed through brittle pages.

"Hey, Alan?"

"Yeah?"

"You think it's weird? That I get tired?"

"But you're not tired."

"But I do get tired. You know? Like last night. How come my android body gets tired?"

I opened my eyes and looked at her. "Because somehow, you're still in there, Bek. And we'll figure it out. We're almost there. Just a few more days. I honestly think the answer we're looking for is on that planet."

She nodded once. I closed my eyes again. She turned a few more pages.

"Alan?"

"Yeah?"

"What if I don't like the answer?"

I slowly closed her book and carefully lowered it to the floor. "C'mere," I said, patting my chest.

She rested her head on my chest and fell asleep before I did.

17

Secret Door

Despite the pesky insects, uncomfortable furniture, and cramped living quarters, the final three days on the Roach were among the best days of my life. Bek and I had nothing to do but get to know each other better. We talked about movies. Childhoods. Bold dreams and bad decisions. Old lovers, failed marriages, and past lives. And every night, we held each other, as the tiny cot would allow for nothing less.

We watched the Firefly movie, Serenity, and grieved again with the crew. Helped them maintain their ship, even assisted with changing its diaper. Shared lasagna with them at dinner, passed the afternoons playing poker. Not that we had any more goola to wager—they already had my island, so the chips were mere funny money. Winner got to pick the next movie.

Shifty won every time. Of all the crew, I trusted him the least. Not that I trusted any of them, entirely. That was Rule #3, after all: Don't trust anybody. But I had to admit, I'd let my guard down a little. What more did we have that they could take from us?

Still, there was my gut, and my gut was reminding me I couldn't be too careful. Every now and then, I'd have Listic hide in a corner and I'd observe the crew on my wristscreen. In such cases, their conversations would be mundane and casual, yet stilted. As though they knew I was watching. So despite the pleasure of Bek's company, I couldn't relax entirely.

There's alway something. Life has a way of keeping you on the periphery of perfection. It's no wonder so many religions claim heaven, peace, or nirvana are unattainable until you transcend this life. Or die.

The fifth day eventually arrived, and with it, our destination. All five of us were crammed into the bridge as the system pulled into view. It was a small system with only four planets and a dying sun. I secretly looked over at Bek, and she nodded. This was it.

Captain Scar belted a few orders pertaining to angle and velocity, but it was obvious his crew was already on top of it. The Roach zipped past the outer planets, honed in on the brown one nearest the sun, and slid into its orbit like a foot into a soft slipper.

Another blip appeared on their system radar. Another body orbiting the planet.

"What's that?" Bek asked, pointing over Topknot's shoulder to the monitor.

Topknot looked quickly at its readings. "That's your poppa's raider ship," she said. "You want us to dock?"

Bek gave me a wary glance unseen by the crew. "N-no," she stammered. "I mean, not yet. Maybe after? After we visit the planet itself. I need to visit the place where he died."

"You say you know where you wanna drop?" Scar asked.

"I do," Bek said. Despite not knowing where this system was with respect to galactic coordinates, that much, she remembered. "Here, I wrote down the location, latitude and longitude." She handed him a page torn from the book she'd been reading, her handwriting scrawled in its margin. "We'll suit up and squeeze into one of your drop ships. Tell me when we're above that point, and I'll hit the big red button you showed me."

"Will do."

"Remember not to leave us behind," I said.

"Don't worry, Blades. Fifty million goola gets you there AND back." Scar shrugged, "Besides, why would I leave behind a perfectly good drop ship?"

I nodded apprehensively, then followed Bek down to the terrasuit closet. She was down to her underwear and sliding the onesie on in seconds. "Oh my god, oh my god, oh my god. Can you believe this?"

"I can," I said, taking off my shirt.

"Well, I can't. I'm finally going to get to see it, again. An ancient civilization. Aliens, Alan! Aliens!"

"Okay, okay, keep it down. Remember, these guys think you're going down there to pay respect to your dead raider father. You need to act... remorseful."

"Remorseful?"

"Solemn. Thoughtful, at the least. Put yourself into your fake self's shoes."

"Right. I know, I know. Sorry, game face. How's this?"

She finished zipping up her suit and waved a hand past her face, changing her expression to...

"I'd say that's 'pensive.' You don't want pensive. You want solemn."

"Pensive, solemn, thoughtful... Like it'll matter with the helmet on." She put said helmet on and sealed it to the suit's turtleneck, and I had to admit, she was right. I no longer had a clue what her expression was.

I caught up with her wardrobe change and grabbed my own helmet. "Well at least try not to walk like you're excited."

"Whatever, Alan. Let's get in the drop ship."

She went in first, and I was right behind her. The name "Shuttlebug" was on a placard next to the hatch. I turned around to close Shuttlebug's hatch behind us and was ready to let go of my concern when I saw a shadow move from around the corner. Rule #11 for being a good private detective: Always keep an eye out for shadows.

I wanted to pass this shadow off as a cockroach, but that damn gut of mine, I couldn't convince myself. That shadow was no cockroach.

It was far too shifty.

· • ·

The drop ship only hung from the Roach's belly for a few minutes before we'd reached the coordinates and Bek slammed the button. Ca-chunk. Goodbye, lasagna.

I could always handle lift offs better than drops. Lift offs involved hurtling toward the void. Drops involved hurtling toward a giant rock.

As we neared the surface, antigravity and hover pads kicked in, cushioning our landing. That part was soft, to be honest. But the damage was already done, and there was a fat wet lasagna noodle on the inside of my visor.

"You said when we go to the Land Before Time, we won't need to wear our helmets anymore?"

"Absolutely not." She unfastened her seatbelt and walked toward the hatch. "I'm telling you, it's like being in a naturally formed terradome. It's incredible. We might as well be on New Gaia. Or Ruvellia. Or Earth." She was about to hit the button. "That is, if Earth had a rock ceiling."

"Hey Bek, wait up."

She turned back to me. "You need help with your seatbelt?"

"No, I just need to tell you. I think I saw something right before I closed that hatch. I think Shifty was following us. He may have heard our exchange. In the changing room."

"Oh. Well, shit." She plopped back down. "Sorry, Alan. You were right. I got too excited."

"What's done is done."

"What do you think they're going to do?"

"Don't know. They could follow us. Or interrogate us. I don't see any reason for them to strand us, though."

She was suddenly exasperated. "Why didn't you tell me before I pressed the button?"

"Would it have kept you from pressing the button?"

She took a deep breath. "No. No, I suppose it wouldn't have."

"So we'll play this out. See how the cards fall, then decide to bluff, call, or fold when the time comes." I stood up and offered her my hand.

She took it and stood up again. "My god, we played way too much poker on that ship."

"We really did."

She opened the hatch and we stepped out onto the rocky soil of planet XR-715, now known as Tudyk. We had landed in the epicenter of a crater that must have been at least ten miles in diameter, the heart of an asteroid impact that occurred millennia ago. Despite the noodle in my face, I could still see okay. I slowly turned around in a circle to take in the view. Everywhere, five miles out, a cliff. Completely barren from here to there but for two formations: One, a mound of rocks that harbored a cave. The entrance to the underworld. The other, a dropship, similar to to the Shuttlebug, but with warpaint markings.

"That must have been the raider's dropship," I said. "The ones that attacked you and your team. Over a hundred years ago."

"And it's still here?" she asked nervously. She turned to look at me, the significance implied within the silence. Their starship had never left the planet's orbit. And if their dropship was still here?

They never left the planet itself.

· ● ·

The cave didn't go far. There were a couple branches, but it was by no means a maze. It was more like a neanderthal's home, with a few alcoves that could easily serve as bedrooms. But there were no stairwells or elevators or deep-set tunnels. There wasn't even a drainage pipe. There was nothing that went down.

Listic lit our way. Bek was getting frustrated at one particular dead end, feeling her hands along the cave wall as though she was trying to claw her way through. I tried to console her, but the last thing she wanted was my hand on her shoulder.

"It's supposed to be here, Alan. God dammit, it's supposed to be here!" More feeling up the wall. "I'm telling you, when you see it? It'll be amazing. Blinding. You'll see."

Listic hovered near my ear and whispered. "And people think I'm the crazy one."

I hated to admit it, but Bek sounded more than excited. She transitioned from anxious to frantic to desperate within ten minutes. At this point, she was indeed bordering on crazy.

Not that I could blame her. All this way, only to find a dead end? This must have been the wrong cave. But no, that was impossible. This formation was unique.

She hadn't been here for over a hundred years. Did the entrance cave in? No, if that were the case, the walls wouldn't be so smooth. There would be rocks and rubble, a tiny indoor avalanche...

I started feeling along the walls. What else was there to do?

Suddenly there was a blinding light. A flash grenade? I couldn't see anything for a moment, but I lunged toward where I knew Bek was standing, an effort to shield her with my body. But instead of an explosion, I heard giddy laughter. Bek's laughter.

I slowly unlocked my eyelids and let the cave come back into view. My eyes must have been playing tricks on me. What I saw was surreal: Bek's arm was merged with the cave wall, sinking into it like it was merely an illusion.

Turned out, it was.

"This is it, Alan! This is the entrance." She pulled her arm back out, closed her eyes, then stuck it back in. Upon submerging it, the room flashed with another brilliant light.

"Jesus, why does it do that?" I squinted my eyes again, tried to blink it off.

"The light thing? I don't know. Richard theorized it was an announcement, or perhaps an alarm system. Come on, follow me." She walked into the wall and disappeared.

Flash.

Great. If the raiders were still here—or rather, if their great, great grandchildren were—I guess they'd know we were coming.

I followed, closing my eyes on the way through. After a beat, I cautiously opened them, expecting to be unable to see anything. And at first, I couldn't. But as my eyes adjusted, I could tell the cave itself was glowing. There was a pink, chalky substance on these inner walls that provided enough light to see by. Listic turned her light off.

Bek took her helmet off and shook out her hair. "That cave wall was more than an illusion. It's a molecular displacement field. Acts as an environmental barrier. You can breath in here."

I took off my own helmet. Bek nodded excitedly at me. In front of us were stairs leading down and to the right. Bek disappeared from sight as she bent around the curve. I followed her down the windy steps, and the path opened up to a wide bluff on the side of a subterranean mountain.

We walked to the edge of the bluff and took it all in. Not twenty feet above us was a rock ceiling, glowing with enough of that pink chalk to spill light onto the flat open valley below. The underground cavern extended to the horizon's vanishing point, no end in sight, hundreds of miles of lush jungle flora beneath a granite canopy. As for fauna? An avian paradise. Brightly colored beaks and feathers fluttered among the trees below. The variety of bird calls were vast, and yet somehow, familiar.

Off in the distance, perhaps two miles out, an anomaly: The tip of a temple could be seen reaching above the palms, and circled wide around it were a pattern of stacked, enormous stones.

It was bad enough I was a detective without a fedora. But now I was a jungle adventurer without a fedora. This was unacceptable.

"Beautiful, isn't it?" she asked.

"Breathtaking." I looked around on the bluff and discovered steps leading down the mountain. "That where we're going?" I gestured to the temple.

She nodded silently. Respectfully. And I followed her down the steps.

As we trekked through the jungle floor, I found myself wanting a machete along with the fedora. The vegetation was so thick, it was slow going. I'd have to inform Alice: Nature's obstacle course put the GC Academy's to shame. Apparently, climbing up and over things was indeed in vogue. These two miles would take us an hour, easy. At first, we tried to go around the branches and leaves and vines and bamboo, but it didn't take long to realize there was no such possibility. It was all branches and leaves and vines and bamboo. There was only over and under and through. Lots of pushing and pulling and climbing and crawling. And a shit load of bird shit.

A bird with the largest beak I'd ever seen pooped on my shoulder while I was straddling a branch, cawed loudly, then flew off, its mission accomplished.

"How much do you know about Earth's history?" Bek asked.

"Enough to know I wouldn't want to live there."

"I wouldn't want to live there, either," Listic said. "And I know all of Earth's history. Want to hear it? 4.54 billion years ago, sixty million years after the formation of Sol, as matter congealed, combined, and coalesced—"

"Maybe another time, Listic," Bek interrupted. "Just saying, we are practically on Earth right now. This jungle environment? It's virtually identical to the one that existed in South America, before the Cluster Migration. Before the Environment Crash. Even some the birds are the same. That friend you made? It's called a toucan."

"Would you like to know the history of the toucan?" Listic offered. "The Keel Beaked Toucan is the most flamboyant bird in—"

"Listic, not now," I said. "Odd as that is, this wouldn't be the first time. The few planets we've discovered with terran-like features in our arm of the galaxy have uncanny similarities. Like those coconut trees on the island I used to own? Pretty much the same as the coconut trees back on Earth, from what I've been told."

"Exactly! It's baffled biologists for centuries. It's been so long since we settled on New Gaia, we've forgotten what a curiosity it is. Our collective conscience, from one generation to the next, gradually accepted the preposterously astronomical odds as common fact, and outside of the scientific community, we've stopped wondering about it. After New Gaia, there was Quartermast. Then Ruvellia. 'Earths,' but not Earth."

She made a good point. As children, we view the universe we are born into with wonder. Everything's a mystery, everything's amazing. But at some point, we become jaded. We're harder to impress. A novelty has to be extraordinary for us to take notice, and even then, it becomes status quo soon enough. We couldn't hold on to that childlike fascination forever.

We couldn't all be like Listic.

"You're right," I said. "Shortly after we discovered Victoria, we took it for granted. Didn't take long. Its significance fell more in the political realm than the scientific."

She reached her arm out to help steady me as I finished crawling over the branch.

"Humans are strange that way. For good or ill, we adapt. We're astonishingly good at rolling with things. Case in point." She made a gesture that encompassed her entire body. "But do you realize how against the odds that is? I mean, of all the directions life could evolve in... For there to be toucans and coconuts on planets that are thousands of light years apart? It doesn't make any sense. Or at least, it didn't make any sense. But that temple?" She pointed in its direction. "It might have the answer."

"Must be some temple."

She smiled. "Just wait and see."

A brilliant light flashed from the subterranean ceiling, so bright it filtered through the canopy of leaves above our heads, like an omnipresent glare. We both winced.

"What the hell was that about?" she said. "We didn't pass through a wall this time."

Another flash. And then a third.

"Three flashes," I said after a moment. "Three flashes, three crew members on the Roach."

"Shit, you're right. They weren't supposed to follow us." She looked at me apprehensively. "You think their intentions are benign?"

I cocked an eyebrow. "I think we better get to the temple before they do."

18

Freaky Temple

The temple reminded me of an Egyptian pyramid, but it had an inlaid staircase leading a third of the way up to a six-foot, vertical slab of rock. Perhaps the building was more Mayan in architectural design, but I didn't know much about such things. Except from what I gleaned from movies, I only knew as much Earth history as they bothered to teach us in grade school. Growing up on New Gaia, you learned New Gaian history. Funny how that worked.

Something I couldn't help but notice, however, was the similarity of the stacked brick structures surrounding this temple to those surrounding the natural arena back on Fillion. The one where I first shot it out with the tall assassin. That couldn't be a coincidence. I was sure Bek would be curious about my observation, but considering we were being hounded by three selfish scavengers with questionable motives, I postponed my disclosure.

We climbed the temple stairs to the six-foot slab. It was framed like a door, but there were no hinges or handles. Even so, I guessed how we'd get in.

"This one's a bit more obvious than the cave in the asteroid crater," Bek said before walking through the slab. Unlike the illusionary cave wall, however, this violation was not accompanied by a flash of light.

Listic and I followed. We found ourselves in a long hallway fashioned of bricks, apparently composed of the same material as the natural ceiling above the underworld. The walls glowed on all sides, as per their job on this funky planet.

"Hold up." I pivoted toward my trusty ORB. "Listic, fly back through that wall and be on the lookout for the Roach crew."

Listic looked at the slab of rock behind us. "What wall?"

"The illusionary wall. The one we just passed through." Listic looked back and forth between me and the wall. "Like we did topside. Oh, for..." I pointed past her. "That wall!"

"That's not a wall, Alan."

"I know. I know it's not really a wall. I'm just calling it—"

"It's a molecular displacement field," Bek interrupted. "Sorry, trying to help."

"Oh!" Listic zipped up and down an inch, her equivalent of a nod. "The molecular displacement field! Got it. Why didn't you call it that, Alan?"

I cleared my throat. "Please go back through the 'molecular displacement field' and look out for the Roach crew. Monitor them and ping me on my wrist monitor when they're close."

"How close?"

"Use your best judgement." I couldn't believe I said that. "And only come back in through that molecular displacement field if you can do it without being spotted. Maybe they won't figure it out. We don't want to make the same mistake we did on the cruiser and guide anyone to our door."

"You got it, Alan." She buzzed through the slab.

Bek and I headed down the hall toward the center of the pyramid. Housed in the middle of the structure was an angular cavern with an enormous dais in the middle, measuring perhaps thirty feet across. Along its circumference were four control consoles made of intricate stonework. Each of them were at waist-level and at a slight angle, so I was only able to fully see the control panel on the console to our right. It was decorated with glyphs and dot-patterns and icons, none of which I recognized, yet somehow intuitive in nature. Some of the stone controls were buttons; others, levers or bars.

I looked back out at the dais. "Beam me up, Scotty."

"Funny you should say that..." Bek smiled.

"Wait a second. A transporter?"

"Better. An interplanetary transporter. Not merely molecular displacement, like the illusionary doors, but quantum molecular displacement. Here, check this out." She flipped a particular series of switches, almost as though she was entering a code, and the stone buttons lit up. "That sequence right there? Weeks of deciphering between me and Jansen. I couldn't have deciphered it without his linguistic aptitude, and he couldn't have deciphered it without my cross-cultural knowledge." She went on to jiggle a couple knobs and toggle a thing-a-ma-jig. A giant holographic planet appeared, hovering over the dais, and equally as wide. As it spun, ever so slowly, I could see what appeared to be oceans and continents, ice caps and lakes. Orbiting the planet like a moon were a collection of symbols and glyphs. Another language, more like a set of hieroglyphics than an alphabet. Probably the planet's name.

And then it hit me. I recognized this planet.

"It's Victoria." I approached the globe and pointed to a spot. "Right here. This little piece of land off the coast of this continent? That was my island." I looked around the room. "How's any of this possible?"

"And check this out. You can flip through the planetarium." She toggled the switch. Another planet showed up.

"There's more?"

"Yep. Lot's more."

I walked around the edge of the dais, counter to the planet's rotation, to see the opposite hemisphere more quickly. "This one I don't recognize..."

"Neither did we. Of course, we didn't recognize the first one, either. Your 'Victoria?' Hadn't been discovered yet. But some of them, we knew." She toggled again. An unfamiliar planet. And again. An unfamiliar planet. And again.

"New Gaia!"

"Bingo. That one, we recognized."

"Well, I used to live there, so..." I paused and rubbed my jaw while she flipped through a few more. Some were darker than others. No... No... "Ruvellia!" No... No... "Quartermast." No... "Holy shit, that's Fillion."

"That's Fillion?" she repeated. The planet was among the darker ones, mostly land with a few giant lakes, the inverse of the more terran planets we'd been cycling through. The lakes were depicted as much larger than they actually were, but their signature was unmistakable. "Interesting. But there's one planet in particular that's even more interesting. Hang on, we're almost there." She kept flipping. "Wait for it…"

"Oh, come on."

"Wait for it…"

Seven planets later, the globe doubled in brightness. An ocean world? But as it turned, I eventually saw a land mass. One giant continent—or giant island, if you took into account all that contention among geologists Listic brought up back at Fillport.

"I don't know this one either," I said. "What makes it special?"

Bek dropped her hand from the panel and stepped back from the console. "That's what we asked. There are fifty-eight planets in the databank, and this one is by far the brightest lit. Perhaps it was the only one unvisited. Or the only one colonized. Or the most recent one colonized. Hell, it could have been the last one that was toggled before the janitor closed shop for the night. That part we never figured out. But we were determined to figure out where it was. We poured through star charts, system archives, planet catalogs… Nothing matched up.

Of course, that wasn't surprising. The odds of tagging it were slim, to say the least. Billions of potential planets in our spiral arm of the galaxy, and the vast majority of them have yet to be surface mapped, even by remote means. Our efforts were more romantic than real. At first, at least. We continued working on other things, too—like deciphering the control panels, exploring the catacombs beneath the temple," she gestured to a tunnel off to the right, its narrow entrance barely noticeable, "but we kept at the idea of discovering this planet for weeks. Months. Finally, Richard realized it wasn't where, but when." She pointed at the globe. The landmass had again rotated into view. "Alan? That continent is Pangaea. That planet is Earth."

"Earth?" I looked around the room again. Acknowledged the intuitiveness of the control panels, the parallels of ancient architecture. "So that could mean... The people who built this were..."

"Humans," she said with reverence. "Humans who went on to populate the Earth. Eons ago. Our ancient ancestors." She cocked her head. "Or..."

"Or?"

"Or maybe the entire opposite. Maybe ancient Earthlings, with technology long since lost, populated this planet. It's hard to say."

My brain was on the verge of exploding out of my ear hole when said ear hole heard an asshole cock a gun from behind the left-most control panel.

"Fascinating," Captain Scar said. "Human aliens. Not that I care." He aimed the gun at me. "What I care about is goola. And something tells me if we cut the legs off of this control unit with a laser, and haul it back to the Roach, and sell it to the highest bidder... goola, baby!"

Bek looked ready to spring at him. "Cut the legs off the— Why you ignorant, good for nothing—"

"Nope!" Shifty interrupted from the other side of the room, cocking a small rifle. "Wouldn't move if I was you."

Bek stopped in frustration and grimaced. "Sorry, Alan. I forgot about the side entrances."

Topknot came in through the main entrance like we had. Listic zipped in from right behind, then flew over her head and ended up a few feet from me. "Alan! Why weren't you looking at your wristscreen?"

Crap. "I'm sorry, you're right. My thoughts were a little occupied with all... this." I wave toward the holographic planet.

"Oh!" Listic said. "Pangaea!"

Bek slumped.

"Alright, enough of the small talk and the apologizing to each other," the captain said. "Far as I'm concerned, you all fucked up. A long time ago. You honestly expected us to believe you'd rather visit the random planet your dad died on rather than the ship he spent his life on? We've known the whole time you weren't being square with us. Didn't take a genius to figure out there was more to this planet than met the eye. Now, tell us what this thing is for."

"Yeah, right." Bek smirked. "I'll let you goons figure it out."

"Okay, let me rephrase that. Tell us what this thing is for, or we blow your fucking brains out."

"To which I respond, I haven't got a brain to blow out. I'm just an android."

"Wait," said Topknot. "No shit?"

"No shit."

"But you look so—"

"I think everyone here is missing the point," Captain Scar interrupted. He honed his gaze on Bek. "Tell us what this thing is for or we blow you up, terminate you, or dismantle you and sell your parts. Pick a phrase."

"You're not going to be doing that," I said. "Because Bek is the only one who knows how to work this thing. If you kill her, you kill your shot at getting any answers."

The Captain looked at Shifty. "Go back to the ship and get the cutting laser. And the chainsaw. Whatever applicable tools we have, all of them."

"Sure thing."

"Okay, wait, hold on," I said. "That has got to be the most colossally stupid idea I've ever heard. If you cut the damn legs out from under this control panel, it's not even going to work anymore. I'll tell you this much: These control panels? They control that glowing planet, there. No control panel, no controlled planet. Understand?"

Topknot looked a little more thoughtful. "What are these planets, anyways? Are they even real places? Your zippy eyeball called that one Pangaea. I never heard of no Pangaea."

"She's got MV, says things. You know that. Point is, if you break the control panel, it ain't worth shit."

"Three more where that one came from," Scar said, gesturing to the other control panels in the room.

"But they're all connected," I replied. I had no idea if this was true or not, but it was time to put my New Gaian grade school science education to work. "You cut one, they all cease working. They form a closed circuit. You idiots know what a circuit is?" They all looked at each other with concern. I went on talking out of my ass. Stalling. Getting them to let their guard down. "Listen, I'm just saying, if you want to make money off this whole thing, there are better ways."

"Like what?" Shifty asked.

"Well..." I casually moved toward the control panel between Shifty and me and, by doing so, closer to the catacomb tunnel Bek had pointed out to me earlier. I gave Bek a look and then flicked my head ever so slightly toward the tunnel's narrow entrance. She nodded quickly.

"Hey, stop moving!" Topknot commanded.

"I was only going to flip a switch on this panel. What I'm trying to say is, if you resold that half of the island I sold you? The one on the beautiful terran planet? You could outright buy this entire planet with that kind of goola. Nobody else knows any of this. From the outside, this is a dead world. You could claim you want to create a way station on it or something. Then, once it's yours, you can pretend to discover this temple and charge admission to the biggest light show in the galaxy."

"You know," Captain Scar said, letting his gun down a little while he scratched his chin, "that's not a bad idea."

I flipped a random switch on the dormant control panel nearest me, but mine didn't light up like Bek's did. Apparently I didn't know the proper sequence. All the same, it did the trick. As soon as Shifty looked down at it, I cracked him upside the face and he fell flat on the floor.

"Now!" I yelled.

Bek tore into the catacomb tunnel, but not before Topknot got off a shot. A bullet snagged Bek's upper arm, bursting it open and leaving her with a dangling assortment of wires and metallic sinews.

I grabbed Shifty's rifle from him and fired a few shots at Scar to keep him occupied. "Listic, Head Butt!" I commanded, pointing at Topknot. Listic took aim and clocked her so hard in the noggin, even I winced. Sympathy pain.

Scar was looking to nail me when I nicked him in the shoulder with my next shot.

"Fuck!" He cowered behind the control panel he was standing behind—which I made sure not to shoot, having made such a big deal about its inherent value.

Shifty got back up after being downed by my face-cracking. He lunged at me, but I whacked him again—this time on the side of his head with the very rifle I'd taken from him.

"Listic, Head Butt the captain!"

I didn't stick around to see how that one played out. Instead, I ran down the catacomb tunnel to check on Bek. The tunnel was darker than up above, with only a few of the inlaid bricks in glow-mode.

I passed three dark rooms on the way to a dimly lit one. The fourth room's entrance looked different than the first few. Its frame was more elaborate, and unlike the others, which were mere openings, this one had a heavy stone door with some kind of ancient control panel next to it. The door had slid mostly into the wall, but I could tell it was there, and that if I were to close it, it would be practically impenetrable.

Bek was waiting for me inside.

. . .

The room itself looked like it served as a temporary sleeping quarters. Along the far wall was a cot, next to it a dead lamp and a small utility box doubling as a nightstand. Near Bek was a huge metal crate fashioned with a bunch of tubes and readout displays, and next to that, some kind of nuclear power generator, humming away. Along the wall closest to me was a collection of six more utility boxes, stacked two-by-two on top of each other with a mirror and a few other nicknacks resting on top of the whole affair, like a makeshift chest of drawers with a vanity. Among the knick-knacks I noticed something that looked like a stand-alone memo recorder, and next to that, an old ORB charging station.

I crouched in the doorway and aimed my gun back toward the catacomb entrance. "Nice call. This is a good position to hold." I noticed a similar control panel next to the door on the inside of the room and reached for it. The buttons were complex. A code was needed. "Hey, do you know how to get this door closed? Looks like we need a—"

"No," she said with calm severity. "We need to leave it open. It was closed, but I used the password to open it."

"Yeah, that's good. But they're going to be barreling down that corridor any moment, and we'd be better off if we could—"

"Please don't close it, Alan." Her eyes looked sad and pleading. "I can't tell you why. I don't even know why. All I know is, you need to leave it open."

"Okaaaaay...."

"This used to be my room." She sounded a little out of it. Too calm. Distant, even. "Back when my team was here. Over a hundred years ago. Just last week." She wiped two fingers on the mirror to acknowledge how much dust had collected. "I need to dust."

Her mechanical arm had been blown off. Was she was going into shock? "You need to take cover, okay? Crouch down behind that large crate."

"You know what's weird? The last thing I remember about being here? I was racing down that hallway from raiders. And what are we doing right now? Racing down that hallway from scavengers. Heh. It's like I'm stuck in some kind of temporal loop. Only my prior memory didn't make it this far." She giggled. "Hey, I think my arm fell off."

"Seriously, Bek. Take cover. Get behind that crate before it's too late."

She walked around to the thing's backside. "You know, this isn't your typical crate. I fucking hate this crate, I do. It's actually a cry—"

"I got 'em! I got 'em!" Listic air-scooted down the hallway and stopped dead in front of me. "Nailed the mother effer, right in that scarred up face of his."

"Atta girl," I said, and patted her.

"Oh, look! A charging station!" Listic floated over to the cradle next to the mirror and settled in. I noticed she had a dent in her. None of us were getting out of this unscathed.

"I don't know if it will work for you, Listic. My cradle may have been specific to my ORB." Bek tapped her temple. "You know, with its IA, and all."

I went over to Bek. I knew I had to guard the door, but I also wanted to check on her arm. Or lack thereof. "Let me look at that..." And I did. Pointless. I was no android repair guy. But then an idea started to bubble up inside of me... "You said you're basically reenacting this scenario, right? You were running from raiders before?"

"Yeah. Weird, right?"

"Is it possible your ORB was in that cradle when they raided? Maybe that's where they stole it from. Before they brought it back to their ship, where the Roach crew found it."

"Maybe, I don't know. Like I said, my memory fades out. But I did take the thing out as often as possible. It helped weaken the signal from my husband—a little, at least. The cyberwear was also in my head, always connected, so no matter what, I couldn't cut the signal entirely. I'd wear an eyepatch when I took it out, did I tell you that? My team called me Pirate Bek..."

"I've had it with you fuckers!" Scar yelled from a few yards down the hallway.

Dammit! Why hadn't Bek let me close the damn door? Was she worried about getting locked inside? Did she suddenly develop claustrophobia? We were fish in a barrel this way.

Scar stumbled into view, rubbing his head as he struggled to remain upright at our room's threshold. Listic either hadn't knocked him out, or he had already recovered. Either way, he wasn't at peak performance. I realized this was my only chance to counter, so I shoved Bek down further behind the crate and aimed the rifle I'd lifted from Shifty at him.

Click went my gun. Just click. Because it was out of ammo.

The captain pulled his trigger as well. Even though his weapon actually hurled death pills, his aim was scattered, no doubt due to his sudden migraine. Bullets flew into the crate. A few more hit the wall right where Bek had been standing. Thank god I'd gotten her down in time. I dove down to join her and was going to tell Listic to head butt him again, despite the futility. There was no way we were getting out of this.

Then I heard the all-too familiar sound of a concussion grenade land in the hallway. And...

Boom!

Parts of Captain Scar splattered all over the room. A finger, and I think an ear, landed on the floor next to my feet, a concave metal plate landed on the cot. A plate from his skull, perhaps? Shit was everywhere. I poked my head up to see where Scar's weapon had landed, ready to lunge for it. But it was still out in the hallway. In pieces.

A few long seconds passed, as did the ringing in my ears. I put Shifty's rifle down on the crate. "Alright, we give up. We don't have any weapons. Don't sh—. Shit, it's you."

Our old friend, the tall athletic assassin, clad in black, marched into the room with his pistol trained on me. I could tell he'd lined up a kill shot. Goodbye, cruel world.

Then he pointed the gun all around. Everywhere except at my face, a complete 360. "Clear!" He stood at attention on one side of the room's entrance.

Another man, dressed in the same garb, came in and stood at attention on the other side of the room's entrance. While they stood there looking sternly at each other, I reached down to help Bek up. She stumbled to her feet, felt heavy. I looked back and forth from one soldier to the other.

"Hey, guys." I didn't really know how to address them. "So, uh... We're good, then?"

A third person marched in between them, his uniform less covert, a little more Fleet-official in design. I recognized the rank on his lapel. All three of them were CyberOps soldiers, and he was their commanding officer. He started to say something, but then stopped himself as he looked at Bek with concern.

"Alan," Bek said weakly. She pulled her only hand from my grip and clutched her stomach. "Alan, I don't feel so good..."

"It's gonna be okay, Bek. These are CyberOps soldiers. If they wanted us dead, we'd be dead already. They're not going to hurt us. Right guys? You're not going to hurt—"

That's when I noticed the blood pouring out of the bullet holes in the crate we'd been hiding behind. Bullet holes created by Scar's wild shooting spree. Blood from the crate, not from me, or from Scar, or from Bek's android body.

I read the crate's label: Cryopod Chamber 054.

The crate wasn't a crate. It was her cryopod chamber. And Bek—the real Bek—was inside of it.

"Alan, I..."

"Bek. No, no, no, no, no, don't do this." I held her android body up. But it was only a puppet. And the puppeteer had been riddled with bullets. "Open the box!" I yelled to anyone who would listen. "Open the goddamn box! She's in there! Her real body's in there!"

"Alan..."

"Bek, I love you. Don't do this, I love you."

She looked at me one last time, offered a wane smile. Her eyes dimmed, and she crumpled to the ground.

19

Case Closed

Rule #12 for being a good private detective: Never get your hopes up.

I was a wreck. The next few days were a fucked up blur, both informationally and emotionally. They'd pulled Bek's real body out of the cryopod chamber and carried her limp form out of the room. I could tell by their expressions she was beyond hope. They gave me some meds because apparently I was hyperventilating. Sedatives. I was out of it for two days, half the time because of the medication, the other half because I was so depressed.

Listic wasn't even around to agitate me into being. That last head butt of hers to Scar's noggin had dinged her up a bit more then usual, and CyberOps technicians were patching her back together. I'd never felt lonelier in my life.

The only thing that helped pull me out of my funk after those first couple of days was a visit from Gina. My ex-GalactiCop partner, now a CyberOps officer, had caught up to the scene and took a personal hand in helping me recover. I don't know what I would have done if she hadn't shown up. I'd never been this devastated before. This was uncharted territory. If I had any access to alcohol, I would have crept into the bottle and lived there, sobriety chips be damned.

I spent time debriefing with Gina and the other agents in one of the catacomb rooms. I debriefed them, they debriefed me. I heard everything they said, but it had little impact on me. I just didn't care, anymore. For what it's worth, here's the whole story.

Right after Bek's anthropology team was taken out by the raiders over a hundred years ago, the scumbags trekked as much shit as they could carry back with them to their dropship. Among that shit was Bek's intimate ansible ORB, which they'd grabbed from the cradle in her room. She must have been sporting her eyepatch at the time.

The raiders shuttled their first batch of loot back up to their main starship, which they'd left orbiting the planet and cloaked, only detectible to them. If they had flown away from the star system at that point, they would have gotten away with the raid, entirely. But being as reliable as your typical criminal, they returned to the scene of the crime—either to steal more shit, or to further investigate the ruins of an ancient civilization.

It was at that time, during the raiders second planetfall, CyberOps arrived on the scene.

CyberOps, given emergency Edgeworld jurisdiction from Fleet, had been tracking this particular raider ship for weeks, slowly closing the gap. These raiders were particularly rancid because they made a point to only raid the most recently colonized of planets. They followed starships that held courses to previously unsettled systems—a scenario Bek's extraterrestrial anthropology team fit the bill for—and then pilfered the settlers before they even had a chance to prop a tent. When the CyberOps starship reached XR-715, however, the raider ship wasn't there—or at least, they couldn't see it, being cloaked, and all. But what they did see was a brilliant flash of light emanating from a deep crater on the planet. And they thought it prudent to investigate.

When CyberOps landed in the crater in their own dropship, they found the raiders' dropship already parked there—the same one Bek and I saw, all these years later. The enhanced soldiers figured out the secret of the illusionary cave entrance in short order thanks to their cybernetic super-senses, marched down the subterranean mountain, and took out the raiders. Retroactive deja vu.

So now, CyberOps knew of XR-715 and its ancient secret. CyberOps, and no one else. And following what in my humble opinion was a warped train of logic, they decided to keep this secret to themselves. Keeping secrets, for the sake of what they called "inter-cluster equilibrium," seemed to be what CyberOps did best. A case of political hubris, if you ask me. I'm not sure they had the right to make such a decision on their own.

All the same, they only knew so much about the temple. Unlike Bek and her team, they never managed to decipher enough runes to turn the teleporter on. They had no idea about the floating holographic array of planets, therefore they never knew what other planets to look in on. For decades, they tried to unlock the temple's secrets, but nadda. All they knew was, based on the architecture's similarity to ancient Earth civilizations, it was somehow linked to our past.

Meanwhile, the abandoned raider starship, cloaked and crewless, kept orbiting dead planet XR-715, going entirely unnoticed—unnoticed, that is, until its cloaking device finally gave out over a century later. It wasn't long after that when our Roach friends discovered it orbiting what's now known as Tudyk. Doing what scavengers do best, they looted it, and in the process acquired Bek's ORB. They then traded her cyberpart, along with a bunch of science equipment, to the guy at the FUC Scrappery, who traded it to some outer-cluster trader, who traded it to the Hack Shack owner on Fillion, who sold it to a John with an ORB fetish.

Bek's ORB had really made the rounds. Not unordinary for tradable cybernetic parts. But it wasn't exactly an ordinary ORB.

The thing about any garden-variety ORB, when integrated into a human head, is the cybernetic upgrade includes a brain-graft component. A socket interface. Bek's and her husband's were no different in that regard. But what made theirs special was the quark integration—the ansible network that allowed them to be in constant communication with each other.

It turned out not only did their ORBs maintain constant communication with each other, but they also maintained constant communication with their hosts, whether the ORB was in the host's eye socket or not. While Bek, the real Bek, was asleep in her cryopod, her ORB, once placed in an android, "woke up." Bek was ghosting the android the whole time. The android provided her real brain, despite being lightyears away, a simulacrum of what it was experiencing, allowing her to feel half alive, but not entirely alive. While her real body slept, she experienced a waking dream as a sexdoll.

It was the same technology that provided me with immediate communication with Alice on my quarkphone, despite the staggering interstellar distance. Yet such a function had never been applied to it this way before. Or since.

As for why Bek wasn't aware her body was in the cryopod in the first place? The aforementioned potential memory loss cryopods often induce. Such side effects were known to occur when hibernation chambers were used, making them loathed by many and now rarely employed. But her intense revulsion for the contraptions was based on more than mere rumors about their short comings; it was based on the fact she was frozen inside one, and didn't even remember climbing in. A subconscious reaction manifesting in a remote controlled body. The same could probably be said for why she was so adamant that I didn't close the heavy stone door to her catacomb chamber. The fact she was buried alive was buried deep in her head.

Ironically, much of this information came from Bek herself. From the memo recorder I had noticed on her makeshift dresser in her catacomb room. Knowing the potential to forget everything, she recorded a memo to herself before going to sleep. The CyberOps team let me listen to it. She explained the events of the last day or so in a frenzied voice: How the raiders had attacked this planet. How her and Eddie escaped into the jungle when the raiders first attacked, which amounted to the last thing she actually remembered upon waking at The Boneyard. But then they crept back into the temple and hid in her room, locking the heavy stone door behind them, only to discover the raiders had already looted a number of things, including her ORB. How they waited for hours until Eddie finally convinced her to use the cryopod if he went back outside to try to take down the remaining raiders before the others came back, assuming they would. How she waited for him even more hours on end, the longest hours of her life.

She hoped her ex-husband might send help her way, since he was always synced to her experiences. But she went on to acknowledge how unlikely this would be since he'd spent the last forty-eight hours hopped up on drugs at a real-girl brothel and may therefore not even remember any of this.

She had no idea what had transpired outside her room. No idea Eddie had died at the hands of the raiders, or that the raiders then died at the hands of the CyberOps soldiers. She was too terrified to open the door, yet because she was the only one left alive who knew how to unlock this door, if she left it closed, no one may ever be able reach her.

In the end, she had little choice. She convinced herself to record a voice memo, climb into a box, and go to sleep. Potentially, forever.

Memory loss from cryosleep varied in nature, but the memories most often lost involved the most recent hours before going to sleep—or perhaps more accurately, the most recent cognizant hours before being reawoken. I recalled rebooting Bek in my apartment back on Fillion, how she'd forgotten we'd already watched Star Wars, how she'd woken up feeling cold and isolated. The clue was there for me to grab, but I didn't pick it up. Clues can be elusive that way—they often go unnoticed when you don't know what you're aiming to prove.

Time passed while Bek hibernated. Decades. Despite throwing in the towel on solving the planet's mysterious origin, CyberOps continued to loosely monitor Tudyk, keeping it in the shadows, unclaimed and unsought. Gatekeepers. Whenever someone stumbled across it, or started collecting bread crumbs as to its significance, they'd "remove" the person from the equation. Like the Hack Shack owner, and, almost, like me.

Turned out Gina caught wind I was involved in all this shortly after their assassin started tailing me back on Fillion. Like an angel from afar, she gave him the word: Don't kill this guy, he's cool. That's why, back in the thunderdome, the guy never shot me despite his cyber-targeting enhancements, why he went easy on me with that delayed grenade lob, why he only wrecked my hoverbike rather than me. I suppose he'd had enough of my shenanigans by the time Mickey settled into the FUC, but even in the Baccarin casino, I don't think he would have killed me. He was just having a bad day. His name was Jim.

Gina admitted Jim's actions were overkill back at the Hack Shack, though. He had a nasty habit of unnecessarily shooting people in the head. The guy had acquired a lot of demerits over the years and was sure to face suspension once they returned to Quartermast.

In any case, when I asked Gina and Jim what took them so long to save our asses out here on Tudyk, or for that matter, why CyberOps hadn't stationed a few permanent soldiers on the planet itself, their answer was simple and simultaneous.

Budget cuts.

These budget cuts must have also pertained to their quarkphone text fund. I gave Gina a hard time about the message she tried to convey: DO NOT FOLLOW TRANSMISSION. REMAIN ON PLANET. I mean really, how the fuck was I supposed to know what to do with that nugget? Turned out CyberOps had detected the ever-present quark signal being cycled from Tudyk to Fillion on some kind of fancy anisible monitoring device of theirs. They sent Jim to Fillion to check it out and shut it down. Bread crumb clean up.

Gina said she figured I already stumbled on to what Bek's ORB was capable of, "being a detective, and all," and she expected me to hold tight until she could reach Fillion and explain it all in person. Providing such explanations to civilians was frowned upon by CyberOps, who'd rather simply have me eliminated. Gina called in all her favors to keep me alive. But by the time she reached Fillion, Bek and I were already gone, leaving Jim to further the chase.

I couldn't entirely excuse myself for not deducing enough to decipher her message. But I did make the helpful recommendation they increase their department's texting budget. Another sentence would have done wonders. Even an emoji would have been nice.

In any case, it all made sense now. All the pieces of the puzzle fit into place. Mystery, solved.

But I didn't care. Whenever our debriefings came to a close, and I found myself alone in an alien room, none of it mattered to me. None of it at all. All I could think about was Bek. And that she was gone. And the sheer irony that I tried to save her by insisting she take cover behind the very box that she ended up dying inside of.

· • ·

One of the CyberOps agents sat me down in one of the catacomb rooms—the one they'd dedicated to all our debriefs. Gina was already waiting there, that cybernetic, bombshell body of hers a little more casually dressed than usual today. She said they only had a few more questions for me, then I'd be free to go.

As though I had anywhere I needed to be.

Jim came in the room soon after, held three coffees and set them down on the table. He apologized for not having any peanut butter and jelly sandwiches on hand—an inside joke, hah, hah—then left again. Gina pushed a coffee my way and took one for herself.

"Tell me about her," she said, then took a sip.

I took a deep breath. One last debriefing. Why not. "What else do you want to know? She never told me how those ancient devices worked. I honestly don't think she knew herself. She was up front with me about everything, and I've been up front with you guys about—"

"No," Gina said softly. "I mean, tell me about her." She reached over and squeezed my shoulder. "How you felt about her."

"Oh."

She offered a sympathetic smile as she leaned back in her chair. She was asking as a friend, now. No longer as a CyberOps officer. She waited for me to continue. She waited until I was ready.

Something caught in my throat when I tried to talk. I'd never found it so hard to talk. But I took a deep breath and tried again.

"She was beautiful," I said.

Gina nodded. Blew on her coffee.

I went on. "I mean, the sexdoll body she was looped up in? It was attractive, sure. Even I'd admit that. No one even knew she was a doll, she'd have to tell them. But that wasn't it. She was beautiful on the inside. And that's what came through. That's what allowed me to believe her. Smart, witty, passionate about life. About anthropology." I laughed. "About movies."

"Heh." Gina nodded. "She sounds like your type, alright."

"She was. She really was. And I thought... You know, I actually found myself thinking... Maybe she's the one? Maybe this could work. Even if she was—god, I can't believe I'm saying this, but even if she turned out to be an android, entirely an android—I thought maybe we could make it work." I swallowed hard. "That's silly, isn't it?"

"I don't think so." She tilted her head. "Listen. I've known you a long time, Alan Blades. I know you've been through a lot. And I know you've always trusted your gut. But this time, well..." She paused for a deep breath. "It was nice to see you trust your heart."

My eyes got foggy. I wiped at them and tried to recover my composition. "This whole thing started at The Boneyard, can you believe that? Bone asking me to track down his rogue doll with the 'ManiAc Virus.'

I knew there was never a ManiAc Virus. At least that much I knew. But look where this all ended up." I stared at the table. "Look who she turned out to be."

We sat there a moment. I didn't know what else to say. Eventually, I took a sip from my own coffee and nodded toward the unclaimed, third mug Jim had deposited on the table. "Jim coming back in?"

"No," Gina said. "That cup is for someone else." She nodded to someone around the corner of the doorway.

A redhead walked in, petite and freckled and pale. She had dimples when she smiled, and excitement in her watery eyes. "Hi, Alan." A tear fell down her cheek. And then in a softer voice. "It's me."

I don't remember standing up from my chair or walking around the table, but there I was, holding her in my arms while my tears met with hers.

I was holding Bek. I was a blubbering wreck of a man, but I was holding Bek, and the universe was worth living in, again.

"It's me, Alan," Bek whispered. "I'm here. I'm really here. Shhh... It's okay, I'm here."

Gina squeezed my shoulder on the way out of the room. I continued hugging Bek until my arms gave out. Once I'd caught my breath, I held her out by her shoulders. "Look at you," I choked. "Flesh and blood."

"I know, right?" She let out a laugh. "Well, not entirely." She patted the place on her waist I'd seen her android-self hold before she collapsed. The place where her real body had been shot while in the cryopod. It sounded vaguely synthetic. "Cyber kidney, cyber stomach, cyber waist patch... These CyberOps doctors know what they're doing. And the best part? They say with these new doodads I can eat as much chocolate as I want and I won't suffer a sugar crash!"

I laughed. We sat down at the table together and took our coffees in our hands.

She took a long sip and closed her eyes. "Oh god, how I've missed that. The real, full taste of coffee."

I nodded, and took a sip of my own. It was the best tasting coffee I'd ever had.

Rule #13: To hell with Rule #12.

20

An Epilogue

"An open marriage," Ernie said. "Can you believe it?"

12 p.m. found me and Bek scarfing down crackdogs at Ernie's vending cart. She'd agreed to meet me there for lunch during our respective breaks—mine from my detective office, hers from her new job as the Extraterrestrial Anthropology Professor at Fillion Edgeworld University. FEU was dying to have her, and she was dying to catch up on the latest research.

CyberOps had let us go, despite knowing what we knew about Tudyk. This was a stark exception to their rule, and only thanks to Gina. It was good to have friends in high places. The only caveats were we were to keep our mouths shut about the planet and its ancient civilization, and Bek had to report any further progress with regard to deciphering the ancient language directly to CyberOps. She also had to report any discoveries she made about Fillion's own ancient ruins. Because that was exactly what the thunderdome arena at the base of Mt. Zelazny turned out to be:

Another gateway left behind by humankind's apparent forefathers.

The idea we were helping CyberOps keep such a large secret from literally everyone else in the human race didn't sit well with me. This was twice now I'd been made aware of Big Deals the clandestine organization was hoarding for itself, the first being the ability for ships to be tracked even while they were in subspace—a potential inter-cluster game-changer I gleaned during my escapades on the Orion Express. It was only my faith in Gina that convinced me to trust them with such secrets.

Bek and I had been back on Fillion for a few weeks, but this was the first time I'd visited Ernie since returning, and he was filling me in on the end result of Orange Lipstick and her affair. Bek looked back and forth between the two of us with raised eyebrows, soaking it all in.

"An open marriage," I repeated. "No shit."

"No shit. So her husband's now sleeping with her cousin, and she's still sleeping with this guy, and they're still sleeping with each other. Everybody's sleepin' with everybody. Just not at the same time." He looked suddenly thoughtful. "Least, I don't think at the same time. Anyways, they're all happy about it. She comes by and tells me the latest whenever she visits him." He gestured to the nearby apartment complex. "Says she owes it all to you."

Bek looked at me with an amused expression. "Congratulations?"

"Heh. Yeah, thanks. I guess." I shook my head. "I tell ya, you leave a planet for a couple of weeks, whole place turns upside down."

"Ain't that the way?" Ernie mused. He pulled out a few napkins from below his cart's counter and started stuffing them into his dispenser. "Oh, that reminds me. Upside-down things, and all. Whatever happened to that killer sexdoll you was huntin' last time I saw you? You ever find her?"

Bek froze with her crackdog held inches from her mouth. Her eyes darted to mine.

"Oh, ah. Yeah." I cleared my throat. "Yeah, I ended up finding her at the edge of the dome. In a terraformer plant. I dropped her off at the GC precinct. Turned out it wasn't the doll at all, just the ORB the guy put in her."

Which wasn't a lie. Including the part about me dropping the doll off—after bringing it back from Tudyk, that is, sans arm and ORB. I told Conner and Lexi I'd found it out there days later, after a more thorough search. Suggested maybe somebody shot it and stole its ORB. They didn't believe me for a second, of course. But they checked the doll for any viruses and found none, and had no reason to press charges against me. If anything, I'd solved their case. It turned out even the guy who we all thought Bek killed made it out alive. So they let me go. Even let Bone have his doll back. He'd since re-marketed Gwen as "dangerously kinky."

Bek looked over at Ernie and tried to play it cool. "Hey, ah... So Alan told me about that case. Is it true what they said about the guy she was with at The Boneyard?"

"Now, that part, I know!" he said. "Absolutely true. Doll bit his dick off, but he's okay. Guy came by a few days ago, told me himself: Got one of them cyberdicks. Says it's fantastic."

Bek looked down at her crackdog. "You know, I think I'll take this to go."

"Doggy bag, comin' right up."

"Happy endings all around."

"Speakin' of which, congratulations, you two," Ernie said. "On the whatever this is."

"Thanks, Ernie" I said.

"And an extraordinary pleasure meeting you, young lady." Ernie offered the slightest of bows as he passed her a small white bag. "Welcome to our unbelievably exciting planet."

"Thank you." She bagged her dog and put it in a large canvas bag slung over her shoulder. "Oh! I almost forgot! Alan, I got you this on the way over." She pulled a hat out of the bag. A fedora. "Ta-da!"

"No way."

"Yes, way. Every good detective needs one."

I bent forward and let her place it on my head. Held the brim and tried to look sleuthish.

She laughed. "It's perfect."

"Alright, you two are killin' me here with the cuteness," Ernie said with a half-smile. But then someone behind me caught his eye and he straightened up with concern.

A flood of red and blue lights suddenly engulfed us. GalactiCop lights.

"Hands in the air, Mr. Blades!" a woman's voice said from behind me. "You're under arrest!"

I recognized that voice. I put my hands half up and turned around slowly. "Well look who graduated from the Academy."

"Alan!" Alice shrieked as she bounced over in her lit up GC uniform and hugged me. "You, like, totally fell of the grid! Never call, never text..."

Alice let go and wiped a locket of blue hair away from her face. I cleared my throat. "Bek, this is Alice. My ex-wife's sister. Alice, this is Bek."

"Nice to meet you!" Alice said, standing at full attention and offering a hand.

"Likewise," Bek said. And meant it.

"Hey Alan, what's the deal with you selling your half of the island?" Alice asked. "I was checking my Victorian Zillow account, and for like a week, it was totally sold to this group called Roach, Inc. I mean, Roach, Incorporated? What's up with that? Like, bad enough Gina had to sell her part, but now you? So I was like, what the fuck, you know? Am I going to be living next to cockroaches when I retire? But then I saw you had maybe bought it back, so I was like, oh, thank god, right?"

I was about to explain the new buyer died suddenly, and the land was being returned to me on account of said buyer trying to kill me, although right now it was caught up in probate. But before I could get a word in, Listic zipped into the scene.

"Alice!"

"Listic!"

The two of them squealed. Bek and I exchanged looks.

Listic shivered in place. "Sorry I wasn't here until now, I was flirting with another ORB."

"No problem. Was he cute?"

"Adorable. In that roundish kind of way. I was showing him my new look." She scooted in closer to Alice's eye and rotated slowly. "Notice anything?"

Alice played along. "Hmmm... What am I looking for, exactly?"

"I got a new plate! Upper rear hemisphere. CyberOps took a dent out."

"Nice!"

"I know, right? I like its sheen."

"Very sexy, Listic." Alice then looked over at me as though she suddenly remembered something. "Oh! Alan, Alan, guess what? Wait, I'll tell you. Okay, ready? I've been stationed here! On Fillion! Can you believe it? Here, on your planet."

I swallowed. "Really?"

"Really! Isn't that great? We can see each other, like, all the time, now!"

"That's, uh... Wow, what a surprise. That's... That's great."

Bek looked at us. "I hate to say this, but I've gotta head back to campus. I'll let the two of you catch up."

"Oh, no, no, no," Alice interrupted. "You two lovebirds both go ahead without me. We'll all catch up later. I'm on the beat, you know? Just grabbing a crackdog on the fly." She landed her fist on the cart. "Hit me, Ernie. Extra relish."

"Atta girl," Ernie said. "Comin' right up."

Bek cocked her head. "Wait, how'd you know Alan and I were... I mean, that we are..."

"I'm a GalactiCop, Bek. I see things." Alice gave her a wink as she took a relish-laden crackdog from Ernie. "Catch you later, Alan."

"Sure thing. You'll have to drop by my office sometime."

She took a huge bite and talked with raised eyebrows around a mouthful of meat and bun. "You haffa offish mow?"

"That I do. With a desk and everything."

She gave me a thumbs up and chewed away while Bek and I departed with Listic in toe.

"She's observant," Bek said. "Should make for a good GalactiCop."

I nodded. "It'll be nice to have someone at the Fillion GC who knows what they're doing."

We had a city block to share before we'd need to go our own directions. We'd finish off the afternoons at our day jobs, then meet back up at my place—I mean, our place—for dinner and a movie. Marple loved Bek and let her move in for only a hundred more goola a month. In return, Bek supplied her with a steady stream of homemade pies. Marple knew the whole story. Knew this Bek was that Bek. I figured we might as well tell her. Nothing gets past my landlady, it was only a matter of time. And she knew how to keep a secret.

"So," Bek said.

"So."

"What's on your agenda this afternoon, detective?"

I thought about my calendar. "I've gotta guy coming in to talk to me about how he's being picked on by his boss over at the brick factory. Wants to see if I can help. You?"

"Unbeknownst to my teaching assistants, we're on the verge of deciphering a rune that might be the key to unlocking the interplanetary gateways."

I laughed. "I think yours is better."

She laughed as well. But then she said more seriously, "No. It's not."

"Now why the hell would you say that?"

She shrugged. "I've been thinking. You remember our conversation back at Fillport? When we were waiting to board the shuttle? I was looking at that holomagazine, and I asked you what you were passionate about. What you believed in. You didn't have an answer at the time. Said you'd get back to me."

I was taken a bit aback. I recalled the conversation, but I hadn't given it much thought since. I wasn't exactly ready with an answer, if that's what she was hoping for.

"I remember," I said.

"Don't worry, I'm not tying to put you on the spot. I think I figured out your answer for you, is all."

"Oh, really?" I offered a cautious smile. "And what is it that I believe in?"

"You believe in people," she answered. We had arrived at the corner where our courses deviated and we stopped. She looked me in the eye. "I'd still be sleeping in a box if it wasn't for you. Or on the run in an android body. I mean, who the hell knows how things would have turned out for me? If it wasn't for you. If you hadn't believed in me." She kissed me on the cheek. "You believe in people, Alan. When no one else does." She turned around and headed for campus. "See you later. At home."

I turned around and headed for my office. Listic zipped over to my shoulder.

"That was quite an adventure the three of us had," she said.

"Uh huh."

"Did I tell you I started chronicling them?"

"Started chronicling what?"

"Our adventures! But only the big ones. Like the one that happened with Alice. On the Orion Express."

"Really."

"Hey, every Sherlock needs his Watson. Know what I'm saying, Alan? Know what I'm saying? Do you get what I'm—"

"I know what you're saying."

"Hey, you know what I called the first one? 'Murder on the Orion Express.'"

Sure, I'll play along. "I don't know... I mean, I get it, it's clever. But it sounds kind of proper, doesn't it? Kind of British? I don't see myself as much of a Poirot. More of a Spade." I adjusted my new fedora. "Or a Marlowe, maybe. I wouldn't want people to read the title and get the wrong idea."

"It's catchy, Alan! Trust me, it's gonna fly off the virtual shelves."

I laughed. "Okay, okay. I'll trust you."

"I'm thinking of calling this one—the one about you and Bek—'Raiders of the Lost Quark.' What do you think?"

"Wow. That's pretty good." It was. At least, I thought so. "Gonna be hard to beat."

"I bet I can, though Alan! So many possibilities. Let's see..." She floated up higher and mumbled title options under her breath. Something about whether or not androids dreamt of electric humans. I was sure I'd be hit with more titles later tonight.

I could see my office building down the block.

Couldn't see the sign, of course. I had to admit, Bone's bouncer was right about that. Maybe I should invest in a new one. With my new look. A picture of me wearing my hat. And while I was at it, I might as well change the slogan. I already knew what it would say.

Alan Blades: He'll believe in you.

Acknowledgements

Writing a novel is by no means a solitary endeavor. I owe enormous gratitude to the following people and organizations:

My pop, Daniel Streeper. Thank you being the first writer I ever knew.

My mom, Kathleen Streeper. Thank you for always believing in me.

My brother, Joshua Streeper. Thank you for helping me shape my imagination.

My long-lost cousin, Len Streeper. Thank you for feedback, guidance, and inspiration.

My primary beta readers, Jessica Kaplan and Yvette Keller. Thank you for suffering through the entire original, frenzied NaNoWriMo draft and helping me shape it into something better.

My publisher and forever friend, Daphne Garlick. Thank you for being my final content editor and for giving yet another Alan Blades Adventure that refined look of a professional product.

My cover artist, Dharitha "Dee" Pathirana. Thank you for bringing my characters to life.

My monthly writing group: Jeremy Gold, Calla Gold, Christine Logsdon, Rachael Quisel, Angela Borda, Lisa Lamb, Kelly Giles, Sharon Whatley, Sia Morhardt, Mark Bessey, Kara Mae Brown, and Melissa Wright. Thank you for helping me put more polish on my prose.

My cheerleaders. Thank you, my friends, for your support and positivity. I am grateful to have you in my life.

My dog, Rufus. Thank you for your unconditional love and constant companionship.

My cats, Ellie and Finnegan. Thank you for sitting on my keyboard and reminding me to chill. Kitty, we miss you. May you rest in peace.

My kick-starter, National Novel Writing Month. Thank you for inspiring this novel's first draft. Again.

My mentors from the Santa Barbara Writers Conference. Thank you for immersing me in the craft.

My primary sources of inspiration: Raymond Chandler, Agatha Christie, Douglas Adams, Ernest Cline, Dashiell Hammett, Ursula K. Le Guin, Philip K. Dick, William Gibson, Jack McDevitt, Roger Zelazny, Walt Disney, George Lucas, Steven Spielberg, Joss Whedon, Ridley Scott, Gene Roddenberry, Roland Emmerich… and all the other giants whose shoulders I am so obviously standing on. Thank you for giving my life direction. I couldn't have done this without you.

Alan Blades #1: Murder on the Orion Express (2017)
Alan Blades #2: The Big Cryosleep (2020)
Alan Blades #3: Coming in 2023!

Nate Streeper is a writer who seeks to entertain his readers with fun fiction laced with the occasional thought-nugget. Located in Santa Barbara, California, he spends his free time running along the waterfront, reading science fiction, creating wacky card games, playing his Xbox, collecting comic books, binging Netflix, walking his dog, petting his cats, and writing... eventually writing.

. • .

www.natestreeper.com

Made in the USA
Middletown, DE
15 November 2020